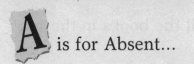 is for Absent...

"Come on!" Dink dragged his friends down the street to the Book Nook.

They looked through the window, out of breath. The bookstore was crowded with kids. The Book Nook's owner, Mr. Paskey, had set up folding chairs. Dink noticed that most of them were already taken.

Dink saw Mr. Paskey sitting behind a table. A big white sign on the table said WELCOME, WALLIS WALLACE!

But the chair behind the sign was empty. Dink gulped and stared at the empty seat.

Where was Wallis Wallace?

Collect all the books in the

A to Z Mysteries™

series!

The Absent Author

The Bald Bandit

This book is dedicated to Lori Haskins
–R.R.

To Kathie, Jesse, and Molly
–J.S.G.

ISBN-13: 978-0-590-81918-3
ISBN-10: 0-590-81918-6

Text copyright © 1997 by Ron Roy.
Illustrations copyright © 1997 by John Steven Gurney.
All rights reserved. Published by Scholastic Inc.,
557 Broadway, New York, NY 10012, by arrangement with
Random House Children's Books, a division of Random House, Inc.
A TO Z MYSTERIES and the A to Z Mysteries colophon are registered
trademarks of Random House, Inc. SCHOLASTIC and associated logos
are trademarks and/or registered trademarks of Scholastic Inc.

36 35 34   9 10 11 12 13/0

Printed in the U.S.A.   40

First Scholastic printing, September 1998

A to Z Mysteries™

The Absent Author

by Ron Roy

illustrated by
John Steven Gurney

SCHOLASTIC INC.

New York Toronto London Auckland Sydney
Mexico City New Delhi Hong Kong Buenos Aires

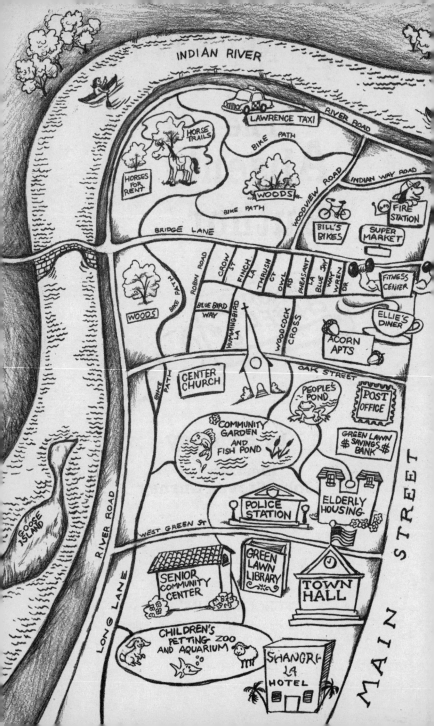

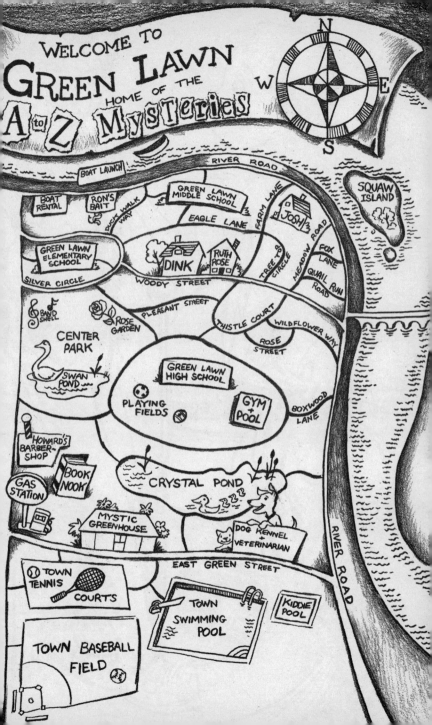

Chapter 1

"Please, Josh," Dink said. "If you come with me today, I'll owe you one. Just name it. *Anything!*"

Dink's full name was David Donald Duncan. But no one in Green Lawn ever called him that. Except his mother, when she meant business.

Josh Pinto grinned at his best friend.

"Anything?" He raised his mischievous green eyes toward the ceiling of Dink's bedroom. "Let's see, what do you have that I want?" He scratched his head. "I know, I'll take Loretta!"

Dink tossed a pillow at Josh. "When I said *anything,* I meant anything but my guinea pig! Are you coming with me or not? I have to be at the Book Nook in fifteen minutes!"

Dink rushed into the bathroom, tucking his shirt into his jeans at the same time. Josh followed him.

Standing in front of the mirror, Dink yanked a brush through his thick blond hair. "Well?" he asked. "Are you coming with me?"

"What's so important about this writer guy?" Josh asked, sitting on the edge of the bathtub.

Dink turned around and pointed his hairbrush. "Wallis Wallace isn't just some writer guy, Josh. He's the most famous mystery writer in the world! All the kids read his books. Except for you."

"If he's so famous, why's he coming to dinky little Green Lawn?"

Dink charged back into his bedroom. "I told you! He's coming because I *invited* him. I'm scared to death to meet someone so famous. I don't even know what you're supposed to say to an author!"

Dink dived under his bed and backed out again with his sneakers. "Please come with me?"

Josh leaned in the bedroom doorway. "Sure I'll come, you dope. I'm just trying to make you sweat. Usually you're so calm!"

Dink stared at his friend. "You will? Thanks! I can't believe Wallis Wallace is really coming. When I wrote and asked him, I never thought he'd say yes."

Dink yanked his backpack out of his closet. "Pack my books, okay? I'm getting Wallis Wallace to sign them all!"

Josh began pulling Wallis Wallace books off Dink's bookshelf. "Geez, how many do you have?"

"Every one he's written." Dink sat on the floor to tie his sneakers. "Twenty-three so far. You should read some of them, Josh."

Josh picked out *The Poisoned Pond* and read the back cover. "Hey, cool! It says here that Wallis Wallace lives in a castle in Maine! Wouldn't that be neat?"

Dink grinned. "When I'm a famous writer, you can live in my castle, Josh."

"No way. When I'm a famous *artist*, you can live in *my* castle. Down in the basement!"

Josh picked up *The Riddle in the River*. "What's this guy look like?" he

asked. "And how come his picture isn't on any of these books?"

"I wondered about that, too," Dink said. "I sent him one of my school pictures and asked for one of him. But when I got his letter, there was no picture."

He finished tying his laces. "Maybe Wallis Wallace just doesn't like having his picture taken."

Josh squeezed all twenty-three books into Dink's pack. He grinned at Dink. "Or maybe he's just too ugly."

Dink laughed. "Gee, Josh, *you're* ugly and you love having your picture taken."

"Haw, haw." Josh picked up his drawing pad. "But just because you're my best friend, I'll draw his picture at the bookstore."

Dink looked at his watch. "Yikes!" he said. "We have to pick up Ruth Rose in one minute!" He tore into the bathroom and started brushing his teeth.

"How'd you get her to come?" Josh called.

Dink rushed back into his room, wiping toothpaste from his mouth. "You kidding? Ruth Rose loves Wallis Wallace's books."

Dink slung his backpack over his shoulder. He and Josh hurried next door to 24 Woody Street. Tiger, Ruth Rose's orange cat, was sitting in the sun on the steps.

Dink pressed the doorbell.

Ruth Rose showed up at the door.

As usual, she was dressed all in one color. Today it was purple. She wore purple coveralls over a purple shirt and had on purple running shoes. A purple baseball cap kept her black curls out of her face.

"Hey," she said. Then she turned

around and screamed into the house. "THE GUYS ARE HERE, MOM. I'M LEAVING!"

Dink and Josh covered their ears.

"Geez, Ruth Rose," Josh said. "I don't know what's louder, your outfit or your voice."

Ruth Rose smiled sweetly at Josh.

"I can't wait until Wallis Wallace signs my book!" she said. She held up a copy of *The Phantom in the Pharmacy*.

"I wonder if Wallis Wallace will read from the new book he's working on," Dink said.

"What's the title?" Ruth Rose asked.

They headed toward the Book Nook.

"I don't know," said Dink. "But he wrote in his letter that he's doing some of the research while he's here in Connecticut."

Dink pulled the letter out of his

pocket. He read it out loud while he walked.

Dear Mr. Duncan,

Thank you for your kind letter. I'm so impressed that you've read all my books! I have good news. I've made arrangements to come to the Book Nook to sign books. I can use part of my time for research. Thanks for your picture. I'm so happy to finally meet one of my most loyal fans. Short of being kidnapped, nothing will stop me from coming!

See you soon,

Wallis Wallace

The letter was signed *Wallis Wallace* in loopy letters. Dink grinned. "Pretty neat, huh?"

"Pretty neat, *Mister* Duncan!" teased Josh.

"You should have that letter framed," Ruth Rose said.

"Great idea!" Dink said.

They passed Howard's Barbershop. Howard waved through his window as they hurried by.

"Come on!" Dink urged as he dragged his friends down the street to the Book Nook.

They looked through the window, out of breath. The bookstore was crowded with kids. The Book Nook's owner, Mr. Paskey, had set up folding chairs. Dink noticed that most of them were already taken.

Dink saw Mr. Paskey sitting behind a table. A big white sign on the table said WELCOME, WALLIS WALLACE!

But the chair behind the sign was empty. Dink gulped and stared at the empty seat.

Where was Wallis Wallace?

Chapter 2

Dink raced into the Book Nook. Josh and Ruth Rose were right behind him. They found three seats behind Tommy Tomko and Eddie Carini.

Dink plopped his pack on the floor. The clock over the cash register said three minutes after eleven.

"Where is he?" Dink whispered to Tommy Tomko.

Tommy turned around. "Beats me. He's not here yet, and Mr. Paskey looks worried."

"What's going on?" Ruth Rose said.

Dink told her and Josh what Tommy had said.

"Paskey does look pretty nervous," Josh whispered.

"Mr. Paskey always looks nervous," Dink whispered back, looking around the room. He saw about thirty kids he knew. Mrs. Davis, Dink's neighbor, was looking at gardening books.

Dink checked out the other grownups in the store. None of them looked like a famous mystery writer.

Mr. Paskey stood up. "Boys and girls, welcome to the Book Nook! Wallis Wallace should be here any second. How many of you have books to be autographed?"

Everyone waved a book in the air.

"Wonderful! I'm sure Wallis Wallace will be happy to know that Green Lawn is a reading town!"

The kids clapped and cheered.

Dink glanced at the clock. Five past eleven. He swallowed, trying to stay calm. Wallis Wallace was late, but it was only by five minutes.

Slowly, five more minutes passed. Dink felt his palms getting damp. *Where* is *Wallis Wallace?* he wondered.

Some of the kids started getting restless. Dink heard one kid say, "Whenever *I'm* late, I get grounded!"

"So where is he?" Josh asked.

Ruth Rose looked at her watch. "It's only ten after," she said. "Famous people are always late."

Now Dink stared at the clock. The big hand jerked forward, paused, then wobbled forward again.

At 11:15, Mr. Paskey stood up again. "I don't understand why Wallis Wallace is late," he said. Dink noticed that his bald head was shiny with sweat. His bow tie was getting a workout.

Mr. Paskey smiled bravely, but his eyes were blinking like crazy through his thick glasses. "Shall we give him a few more minutes?"

The crowd grumbled, but nobody wanted to go anywhere.

Ruth Rose started to read her book.

Josh opened his sketch pad and began drawing Mr. Paskey. Dink turned and stared at the door. He mentally ordered Wallis Wallace to walk through it. *You have to come!* thought Dink.

Ever since he had received Wallis Wallace's letter, he'd thought about only one thing: meeting him today.

Suddenly Dink felt his heart skip a beat. THE LETTER! *Short of being kidnapped,* the letter said *nothing will stop me from coming.*

Kidnapped! Dink shook himself. Of course Wallis Wallace hadn't been kidnapped!

Mr. Paskey stood again, but this time he wasn't smiling. "I'm sorry, kids," he said. "But Wallis Wallace doesn't seem to be coming after all."

The kids groaned. They got up, scraping chairs and bumping knees. Mr. Paskey apologized to them as they crowded past, heading for the door.

"I've read every single one of his books," Dink heard Amy Flower tell another girl. "Now I'll probably *never* meet anyone famous!"

"I can't believe we gave up a soccer game for this!" Tommy Tomko muttered to Eddie Carini on their way out.

Ruth Rose and Josh went next, but Dink remained in his seat. He was too stunned to move.

He felt the letter through his jeans. *Short of being kidnapped...* Finally Dink got up and walked out.

Josh and Ruth Rose were waiting for him.

"What's the matter?" Ruth Rose said. "You look sick!"

"I *am* sick," Dink mumbled. "I invited him here. It's all my fault."

"What's all your fault?" Josh asked.

"This!" he said, thrusting the letter into Josh's hands. "Wallis Wallace has been *kidnapped!*"

Chapter 3

"KIDNAPPED?" Ruth Rose shrieked. Her blue eyes were huge.

Josh and Dink covered their ears.

"Shh!" said Josh. He handed the letter back to Dink and gave a quick gesture with his head. "Some strange woman is watching us!"

Dink had noticed the woman earlier. She'd been sitting in the back of the Book Nook.

"She's coming over here!" Ruth Rose said.

The woman had brown hair up in a neat bun. Half-glasses perched on her nose. She was wearing a brown dress and brown shoes, and carried a book bag with a picture of a moose on the side. Around her neck she wore a red scarf covered with tiny black letters.

"Excuse me," she said in a soft, trembly voice. "Did you say Wallis Wallace has been *kidnapped?*" The woman poked her glasses nervously.

Dink wasn't sure what to say. He *thought* Wallis Wallace had been kidnapped, but he couldn't be sure. Finally he said, "Well, he might have been."

"My goodness!" gasped the woman.

"Who are you?" Josh asked her.

"Oh, pardon me!" The woman blushed. "My name is Mavis Green," she mumbled. "I'm a writer, and I came to meet Mr. Wallace."

Dink said, "I'm Dink Duncan. These are my friends Ruth Rose and Josh."

Mavis shook hands shyly.

Then she reached into her book bag and pulled out a folded paper.

"Wallis Wallace wrote to me last week. He said something very peculiar in his letter. I didn't think much of it at the time. But when he didn't show up today, and then I heard you mention kidnapping..."

She handed the letter to Dink. Josh and Ruth Rose read it over his shoulder.

Dear Mavis,

    Thanks for your note. I'm well, and thank you for asking. But lately my imagination is playing tricks on me. I keep thinking I'm being followed! Maybe that's what happens to mystery writers—we start seeing bad guys in the shadows! At any rate, I'm eager to meet you in Green Lawn, and I look forward to our lunch after the signing.

Wallis Wallace

"Wow!" said Ruth Rose. "First he says he's being followed, and then he winds up missing!"

Dink told Mavis about his letter from Wallis Wallace. "He said the only thing that would keep him from coming today was if he was kidnapped!"

"Oh, dear!" said Mavis. "I just don't understand. Why would anyone want to kidnap Wallis Wallace?"

"If he's the most famous mystery writer in the world, he must be rich, right?" Josh said. "Maybe someone kidnapped him for a ransom!"

Suddenly Josh grabbed Dink and spun him around, pointing toward the street. "Look! The cops are coming! They must have heard about the kidnapping!"

A police officer was walking toward them.

"Josh, that's just Officer Fallon,

Jimmy Fallon's grandfather," said Dink. "Jimmy came to get a book signed. I saw him inside the Book Nook."

"Maybe we should show Officer Fallon these letters," Ruth Rose suggested. "They could be clues if Wallis Wallace has really been kidnapped!"

"Who's been kidnapped?" asked Officer Fallon, who was now standing near them. "Not my grandson, I hope," he added, grinning.

Dink showed Officer Fallon the two letters. "We think Wallis Wallace might have been kidnapped," he said. "He promised he'd come to sign books, but he isn't here."

Officer Fallon read Mavis's letter first, then Dink's. He scratched his chin, then handed the letters back.

"The letters do sound a bit suspicious," he said. "But it's more likely that Mr. Wallace just missed his flight."

Jimmy Fallon ran out of the Book Nook, waving a Wallis Wallace book at his grandfather. "Grampa, he never came! Can we go for ice cream anyway?"

Officer Fallon put a big hand on Jimmy's head. "In a minute, son." To Dink he said, "I wouldn't worry. Mr. Wallace will turn up. Call me tomorrow if there's no news, okay?"

They watched Jimmy and his grandfather walk away.

Dink handed Mavis's letter back to her. He folded his and slid it into his pocket. Crazy thoughts were bouncing around in his head. *What if Wallis Wallace really has been kidnapped? It happened because I invited him to Green Lawn. I'm practically an accomplice!*

"I don't want to wait till tomorrow," he said finally. "I say we start looking for Wallis Wallace now!"

"Where do we start?" Ruth Rose asked.

Dink jerked his thumb over his shoulder. "Right here at the Book Nook."

"Excuse me," Mavis Green said shyly. "May I come along, too?"

"Sure," Dink said. He marched back inside the Book Nook, with the others following.

Mr. Paskey was putting the Wallis Wallace books back on a shelf. He looked even more nervous than before.

"Excuse me, Mr. Paskey," Dink said. "Have you heard from Wallis Wallace?"

Mr. Paskey's hand shot up to his bow tie. "No, Dink, not a word."

"We think he was kidnapped!" Josh said.

Mr. Paskey swallowed, making his bow tie wiggle. "Now, Joshua, let's not jump to conclusions. I'm sure there's a rational explanation for his absence."

Dink told Mr. Paskey about the two letters. "I'm really worried, Mr. Paskey. Where could he be?"

Mr. Paskey took out a handkerchief and wiped his face. "I have no idea." He removed a paper from his desk and handed it to Dink. "All I have is his itinerary."

The others looked over Dink's shoulder as he read:

Itinerary for Wallis Wallace:

1. Arrive at Bradley Airport at
    7:00 P.M., Friday, July 15,
    New England Airlines, Flight 3132.

2. Meet driver from Lawrence
    Taxi Service.

3. Drive to Shangri-La Hotel.

4. Sign books at Book Nook at 11:00 A.M.,
    Saturday, July 16.

5. Lunch, then back to airport for
    4:30 P.M. flight.

"Can I keep this?" Dink asked Mr. Paskey.

Mr. Paskey blinked. "Well, I guess that'll be all right. But why do you need the itinerary?"

Dink picked up a marker and drew circles around the words AIRPORT, TAXI, HOTEL, and BOOK NOOK.

"This is like a trail. It leads from the airport last night to the Book Nook today," Dink said. "Somewhere along this trail, Wallis Wallace disappeared."

Dink stared at the itinerary. "And we're going to find him!"

Chapter 4

Mr. Paskey shooed them out of the Book Nook and locked the front door. "I have to eat lunch," he said. He scurried down Main Street.

"Come on," Dink said. "There's a phone in Ellie's Diner."

"Good, we can eat while you're calling..." Josh stopped. "Who are you calling?"

"The airport," Dink said, "to see if Wallis Wallace was on that seven o'clock flight last night."

They walked into Ellie's Diner just

as Jimmy Fallon and his grandfather came out. Jimmy was working on a triple-decker chocolate cone.

Ellie stood behind the counter. As usual, her apron was smeared with ketchup, mustard, chocolate, and a lot of stuff Dink didn't recognize.

Ellie smiled. "Hi, Dink. Butter crunch, right?"

Dink shook his head. "No, thanks, Ellie. I came to use the phone."

"Excuse me, but would it be all right if I bought you each a cone?" Mavis Green asked. "I was going to buy lunch for Mr. Wallace anyway."

"Gee, thanks," Josh said. "I'll have a scoop of mint chip and a scoop of pistachio."

"Oh, you like green ice cream, too," Mavis said. She smiled shyly. "I'll have the same, please."

"I like pink ice cream," Ruth Rose

said. "I'll have a strawberry cone, please. One scoop."

"How about you, Dink?" Mavis asked.

"I'm not hungry, thanks," he said. "But you guys go ahead. I'm going to call the airport."

Dink felt guilty. If he hadn't invited Wallis Wallace to Green Lawn, his favorite author would be safe at home in his castle in Maine.

But Dink couldn't help feeling excited too. He felt like a detective from one of Wallis Wallace's books!

Dink stepped into the phone booth, looked up the number for New England Airlines, and called. When a voice came on, he asked if Wallis Wallace had been aboard Flight 3132 last night.

"He was? Did it land at seven o'clock?" Dink asked. "Thanks a lot!"

He rushed out of the phone booth. "Hey, guys, they told me Wallis Wallace was on the plane—and it landed right on time!"

"So he didn't miss his flight," Ruth Rose said through strawberry-pink lips.

"That's right!" Dink pulled out the itinerary. He drew a line through AIR-PORT.

"This is so exciting!" Ruth Rose said.

"Now what?" Josh asked, working on his double-dipper.

Dink pointed to his next circle on the itinerary. "Now we need to find out if a taxi picked him up," he said.

"Lawrence Taxi is over by the river," Ruth Rose said.

Dink looked at Mavis. "Would you like to come with us? We can walk there in five minutes."

Mavis Green wiped her lips carefully with a napkin. "I'd love to come," she said in her soft voice.

They left Ellie's Diner, walked left on Bridge Lane, then headed down Woodview Road toward the river.

"Mr. Paskey looked pretty upset, didn't he?" Josh said, crunching the last of his cone. His chin was green.

"Wouldn't you be upset if you had a bunch of customers at your store waiting to meet a famous author and he didn't show up?" Ruth Rose asked.

"Yeah, but he was sweating buckets," Josh said. "I wonder if Mr. Paskey kidnapped Wallis Wallace."

"Josh, get real! Why would Mr.

Paskey kidnap an author?" asked Ruth Rose. "He sells tons of Wallis Wallace's books!"

"I don't think Mr. Paskey is the kidnapper," Dink said. "But in a way, Josh is right. Detectives should consider everyone a suspect, just the way they do in Wallis Wallace's books."

At River Road, they turned left. Two minutes later, Dink pushed open the door of the Lawrence Taxi Service office. He asked the man behind the counter if one of their drivers had met Flight 3132 at Bradley Airport the previous night.

The man ran his finger down a list on a clipboard. "That would be Maureen Higgins. She's out back eating her lunch," he said, pointing over his shoulder. "Walk straight through."

They cut through the building to a grassy area in back. Through the trees,

Dink could see the Indian River. The sun reflected off the water like bright coins.

A woman was sitting at a picnic table eating a sandwich and filling in a crossword puzzle.

"Excuse me, are you Maureen Higgins?" Dink asked.

The woman shook her head without looking up. "Nope, I'm Marilyn Monroe."

The woman wrote in another letter. The she looked up. She had the merriest blue eyes Dink had ever seen.

"Yeah, cutie pie, I'm Maureen." She pointed her sandwich at Dink. "And who might you be?"

"I'm Dink Duncan," he said. "These are my friends Josh, Ruth Rose, and Mavis."

"We wondered if you could help us," Ruth Rose said.

Maureen stared at them. "How?"

"Did you pick up a man named Wallis Wallace at the airport last night?" Dink asked.

Maureen squinted one of her blue eyes. "Why do you want to know?"

"Because he's missing!" said Josh.

"Well, I sure ain't got him!" Maureen took a bite out of her sandwich. Mayonnaise oozed onto her fingers.

"I know. I mean, we didn't think you had him," Dink said. "But did you pick him up?"

Maureen nodded, swallowing. "Sure I picked him up. Seven o'clock sharp, I was there with my sign saying WALLACE. The guy spots me, trots over, I take him out to my taxi. He climbs in, carrying a small suitcase. Kinda spooky guy. Dressed in a hat, long raincoat, sunglasses. Sunglasses at night! Doesn't speak a word, just sits. Spooky!"

"Did you take him to the Shangri-la Hotel?" Dink asked.

"Yep. Those were my orders. Guy didn't have to give directions, but it woulda been nice if he'd said something. Pass the time, you know? Lotta people, they chat just to act friendly. Not this one. Quiet as a mouse in the back seat."

Maureen wiped mayonnaise from her fingers and lips. "Who is this Wallace fella, anyway?"

"He's a famous writer!" Ruth Rose said.

Maureen's mouth fell open. "You mean I had a celebrity in my cab and never even knew it?"

"What happened when you got to the hotel?" Josh asked.

Maureen stood up and tossed her napkin into the trash. "I get out of my side, then I open his door. He hops out,

hands me a twenty. Last I seen, he's scooting into the lobby."

Dink pulled out the itinerary. He crossed out TAXI with a thick black line. Then he drew a question mark next to HOTEL.

"Thanks a lot, Miss Higgins," he said. "Come on, guys, I have a feeling we're getting closer to finding Wallis Wallace."

Maureen put her hand on Dink's arm. "I just thought of something," she said. "When he handed me my fare, this Wallace fella was smiling."

Dink stared at Maureen. "Smiling?"

She nodded. "Yep. Had a silly grin on his face. Like he knew some big secret or something."

Chapter 5

Back on Main Street, Dink adjusted his backpack and led the way to the Shangri-la Hotel.

"Maureen Higgins said she dropped him off at the hotel last night," he told the others, "so that's our next stop."

"What if she didn't?" Josh said, catching up to Dink.

"What do you mean?"

"I mean maybe Maureen Higgins wasn't telling the truth. Maybe *she* kidnapped him!"

"And she's hiding him in her lunch-

box!" Ruth Rose said.

"Very funny, Ruth Rose," Josh said. "Maureen Higgins said she drove Wallis Wallace to the hotel. But what if she drove him somewhere else?"

"You could be right," Dink said. "That's why we're going to the hotel."

With Dink in the lead, the four approached the check-in counter in the hotel lobby.

"Excuse me," Dink said to the man behind the counter.

"May we help you?" He was the saddest-looking man Dink had ever seen. He had thin black hair and droopy eyebrows. His skinny mustache looked like a sleeping centipede. A name tag on his suit coat said MR. LINKLETTER.

"We're looking for someone."

Mr. Linkletter stared at Dink.

"He's supposed to be staying in this hotel," Josh said.

The man twitched his mustache at Josh.

"His name is Wallis Wallace," Dink explained. "Can you tell us if he checked in last night?"

Mr. Linkletter patted his mustache. "Young sir, if we had such a guest, we wouldn't give out any information. We have *rules* at the Shangri-la," he added in a deep, sad voice.

"But he's missing!" Ruth Rose said. "He was supposed to be at the Book Nook this morning and he never showed up!"

Dink pulled out the itinerary. "See, he was coming here from the airport. The taxi driver said she saw him walk into this lobby."

"And he's famous!" Ruth Rose said. She placed her book on the counter in front of Mr. Linkletter. "He wrote this!"

Sighing, Mr. Linkletter looked down

at Ruth Rose. "We are quite aware of who Mr. Wallace is, young miss."

Mr. Linkletter turned his sad eyes back on Dink. He flipped through the hotel register, glanced at it, then quickly shut the book. "Yes, Mr. Wallace checked in," he said. "He arrived at 8:05."

"He did? What happened after that?" Dink asked.

Mr. Linkletter pointed toward a bank of elevators. "He went to his room. We offered to have his suitcase carried, but he preferred to do it himself."

"Have you seen Mr. Wallace yet today?" Mavis asked.

"No, madam, I haven't seen him. Mr. Wallace is still in his room."

Still in his room!

Suddenly Dink felt relieved. He felt a little foolish, too. Wallis Wallace hadn't been kidnapped after all. He was probably in his room right now!

"Can you call him?" Dink asked.

Mr. Linkletter tapped his fingers on the closed hotel register. He patted his mustache and squinted his eyes at Dink.

"Please?" Dink said. "We just want to make sure he's okay."

Finally Mr. Linkletter turned around. He stepped a few feet away and picked up a red telephone.

As soon as his back was turned, Josh grabbed the hotel register. He quickly found yesterday's page. Dink and the others crowded around Josh for a peek.

Dink immediately recognized Wallis Wallace's signature, scrawled in big loopy letters. He had checked in to Room 303 at five after eight last night.

Dink pulled out his letter from Wallis Wallace and compared the two

signatures. They were exac†ly the same.

Josh dug his elbow into Dink's side. "Look!" he whispered.

Josh was pointing at the next line in the register. ROOM 302 had been printed there. Check-in time was 8:15.

"Someone else checked in right after

Wallis Wallace!" Ruth Rose whispered.

"But the signature is all smudged," Dink said. "I can't read the name."

When Mr. Linkletter hung up the phone, Josh shoved the register away.

As Mr. Linkletter turned back around, Dink shut the register. He looked up innocently. "Is he in his room?" Dink asked.

"I don't know." Mr. Linkletter tapped his fingers on his mustache. "There was no answer."

Dink's stomach dropped. His mind raced.

If Wallis Wallace had checked into his room last night, why hadn't he shown up at the Book Nook today?

And why wasn't he answering his phone?

Maybe Wallis Wallace had been kidnapped after all!

Chapter 6

Dink stared at Mr. Linkletter. "No answer? Are you sure?"

Mr. Linkletter nodded. He looked puzzled. "Perhaps he's resting and doesn't want to be disturbed."

"Can we go up and see?" Ruth Rose smiled sweetly at Mr. Linkletter. "Then we'd know for sure."

Mr. Linkletter shook his head. "We cannot disturb our guests, young miss. We have *rules* at the Shangri-la. Now good day, and thank you."

Ruth Rose opened her mouth. "But, Mis—"

"Good day," Mr. Linkletter said firmly again.

Dink and the others walked toward the door.

"Something smells fishy," muttered Dink.

"Yeah," Josh said, "and I think it's that Linkletter guy. See how he tried to hide the register? Then he turned his back. Maybe he didn't even call Room 303. Maybe he was warning his partners in crime!"

"What are you suggesting, Josh?" Mavis asked.

"Maybe Mr. Linkletter is the kidnapper," Josh said. "He was the last one to see Wallis Wallace."

A man wearing a red cap tapped Dink on the shoulder. "Excuse me, but I overheard you talking to my boss, Mr.

Linkletter. Maybe I can help you find Wallis Wallace. My kids love his books."

"Great!" Dink said. "Can you get us into his room?"

The man shook his head. "No, but I know the maid who cleaned the third-floor rooms this morning. Maybe she noticed something."

With his back to Mr. Linkletter, the man scribbled a few words on a pad and handed the page to Dink. "Good luck!" the man whispered, and hurried away.

"What'd he write?" Josh asked.

"Outside," Dink said.

They all shoved through the revolving door. In front of the hotel, Dink looked at the piece of paper. "The maid's name is Olivia Nugent. She lives at the Acorn Apartments, Number Four."

"Livvy Nugent? I know her!" Ruth Rose said. "She used to be my baby-sitter."

"The Acorn is right around the corner on Oak Street," Dink said. "Let's go!"

Soon all four were standing in front of Livvy Nugent's door. She answered it with a baby in her arms. Another little kid held on to her leg and stared at Dink and the others. He had peanut butter all over his face and in his hair.

"Hi," the boy's mother said. "I'm not buying any cookies and I already get the *Green Lawn Gazette.*" She was wearing a man's blue shirt and jeans. Her brown hair stuck out from under a Yankees baseball cap.

"Livvy, it's me!" Ruth Rose said.

Olivia stared at Ruth Rose, then broke into a grin.

"Ruth Rose, you're so big! What are

you up to these days?"

"A man at the hotel gave us your name."

"What man?"

"He was sort of old, wearing a red cap," Dink said.

Livvy chuckled. "Freddy old? He's only thirty! So why did he send you to see me?"

"He told us you cleaned the rooms on the third floor this morning," Dink said. "Did you clean Room 303?"

Livvy Nugent shifted the baby to her other arm. "Randy, please stop pulling on Mommy's leg. Why don't you go finish your lunch?" Randy ran back into the apartment.

"No," Livvy told Dink. "Nobody slept in that room. The bed was still made this morning. The towels were still clean and dry. I remember because there were two rooms in a row that I

didn't have to clean—303 and 302.
Room 302 had a Do Not Disturb sign
hanging on the doorknob. So I came
home early, paid off the baby-sitter, and
made our lunches."

"But Mr. Linkletter told us Wallis

Wallace checked into Room 303 last night," Ruth Rose said.

"Not *the* Wallis Wallace? The mystery writer? My kid sister *devours* his books!"

Dink nodded. "He was supposed to sign books at the Book Nook this morning. But he never showed up!"

"We even saw his signature on the hotel register," Ruth Rose said.

"Well, Wallis Wallace might have signed in, but he never slept in that room." Livvy grinned. "Unless he's a ghost."

"I wonder if Mr. Linkletter could have made a mistake about the room number," Mavis suggested quietly.

Livvy smiled at Mavis. "You must not be from around here. Mr. Linkletter *never* makes mistakes."

"So Wallis Wallace signed in, but he didn't sleep in his room," said Dink.

"That means..."

"Someone must have kidnapped him before he went to bed!" Josh said.

Livvy's eyes bugged. "Kidnapped! Geez, Mr. Linkletter will have a fit." She imitated his voice. "We have *rules* about kidnappings at the Shangri-la!"

Everyone except Dink laughed. All he could think about was Wallis Wallace, his favorite author, kidnapped.

Suddenly a crash came from inside the apartment. "Oops, gotta run," Livvy said. "Randy is playing bulldozer with his baby sister's stroller again. I hope you find Wallis Wallace. My kid sister will die if he doesn't write another book!"

They walked slowly back to Main Street. Dink felt as though his brain was spinning around inside his head.

Now he felt certain that Wallis Wallace had been kidnapped.

But who did it? And when?

And where was Wallis Wallace being kept?

"Guys, I'm feeling confused," he said. "Can we just sit somewhere and go over the facts again?"

"Good idea," Josh said. "I always think better when I'm eating."

"I'm feeling a bit peckish, too," Mavis said. "I need a quiet cup of tea and a sandwich. Should we meet again after lunch?"

Ruth Rose looked at her watch. "Let's meet at two o'clock."

"Where?" Josh asked.

"Back at the hotel." Dink peered through the door glass at Mr. Linkletter.

"Unless Maureen Higgins and Mr. Linkletter are *both* lying," he said, "Wallis Wallace walked into the Shangri-la last night—and never came out."

Chapter 7

Dink, Josh, and Ruth Rose left Mavis at Ellie's Diner, then headed for Dink's house. Dink made tuna sandwiches and lemonade. Ruth Rose brought a bag of potato chips and some raisin cookies from her house next door.

They ate at the picnic table in Dink's backyard. Dink took a bite of his sandwich. After he swallowed, he said, "Let's go over what we know."

He moved his lemonade glass to the middle of the table. "My glass is the airport," he said. "We know Wallis Wallace landed."

"How do we *know* he did?" Josh asked.

"The airport told me the plane landed, Josh."

"And Maureen Higgins said she picked him up," Ruth Rose added.

"Okay, so your glass is the airport," Josh said. "Keep going, Dink."

Dink slid his sandwich plate over next to his glass. "My plate is Maureen's taxi." He put a cookie on the plate. "The cookie is Wallis Wallace getting into the taxi."

Dink slid the plate over to the opened potato chip bag. "This bag is the hotel." He walked the Wallis Wallace cookie from the plate into the bag.

Dink looked at Josh and Ruth Rose. "But what happened to Wallis Wallace after he walked into the lobby?"

"I'll tell you what happened," Josh said. He lined up four cookies in a row. "This little cookie is Mr. Paskey. These three are Maureen, Mr. Linkletter, and Olivia Nugent."

Josh looked up and waggled his eyebrows. "I think these four cookies planned the kidnapping *together!*"

Ruth Rose laughed. "Josh, Mr. Paskey and Livvy Nugent are friends of ours. Do you really think they planned this big kidnapping? And can you see Mr. Linkletter and my baby-sitter pulling off a kidnapping together?"

Josh ate a potato chip. "Well, maybe not. But *someone* kidnapped the guy!"

"Our trail led us to the hotel, and then it ended," Dink said. "What I want to know is, if Wallis Wallace isn't in his room, where is he?"

Dink nibbled on a cookie thoughtfully. "I'm getting a headache trying to sort it all out."

Ruth Rose dug in Dink's backpack and brought out three Wallis Wallace books. "I have an idea." She handed books to Dink and Josh and kept one.

"What're these for?" Dink asked.

"Josh made me think of something Wallis Wallace wrote in *The Mystery in the Museum*," Ruth Rose said. "He said the more you know about the victim, the easier it is to figure out who did the crime."

She turned to the back cover of her book. "So let's try to find out more about our victim. Listen to this." She started reading out loud. "'When not writing, the author likes to work in the garden. Naturally, Wallis Wallace's favorite color is green.'"

"Fine," said Josh, "but how does knowing his favorite color help us find him, Ruth Rose?"

"I don't know, but maybe if we read more about him, we'll discover some clues," Ruth Rose said. "What does it say on the back of your book?"

Josh flipped the book over and began

reading. "'Wallis Wallace lives in a castle called Moose Manor.'" He looked up. "We already knew he lived in a castle. I don't see any clues yet, you guys."

Ruth Rose stared at Josh. "You know, something is bugging me, but I can't figure out what it is. Something someone said today, maybe." She shook her head. "Anyway, read yours, Dink."

Dink read from the back cover of his book. "'Wallis Wallace gives money from writing books to help preserve the wild animals that live in Maine.'"

"Okay, he gives money away to save animals, lives in a castle, and grows a bunch of green stuff," Josh said, counting on his fingers. "Still no clues."

Josh took another cookie. "But I just thought of something." He began slowly munching on the cookie.

Dink raised his eyebrows. "Are you going to tell us, Josh?"

"Well, I was thinking about Room 302. Remember, someone signed the register right after Wallis Wallace checked into Room 303? And the signature was all smudged? And then Olivia Nugent—"

"—told us that Room 302 had a Do Not Disturb sign on it!" Ruth Rose interrupted. "Livvy never went into that room at all!"

Just then Dink's mother drove up the driveway. She got out of the car, waved, and started walking toward the picnic table.

"Oh, no!" Dink said. "If Mom finds out I'm trying to find a kidnapper, she won't let me out of the house! Don't say anything, okay?"

"Can't I even say hi?" Josh asked.

Dink threw a potato chip at Josh. "Say hi, then shut up about you-know-what!"

"Hi, Mrs. Duncan!" Josh said, sliding a look at Dink.

"Hi, kids. How was the book signing? Tell me all about Wallis Wallace, Dink. Is he as wonderful as you expected?"

Dink stared at his mother. He didn't want to lie. But if he told her the truth, she wouldn't let him keep looking for Wallis Wallace. And Dink had a sudden feeling that they were very close to finding him.

We can't stop now! he thought. He looked at his mother and grinned stupidly.

"Dink? Honey? Why is your mouth open?"

He closed his mouth. *Think, Dink!* he ordered himself.

Suddenly Josh knocked over his lemonade glass. The sticky cold liquid spilled into Dink's lap.

Dink let out a yowl and jumped up.

"Gee, sorry!" said Josh.

"Paper towels to the rescue!" Dink's mother ran toward the house.

"Good thinking, Josh," Dink said, wiping at his wet jeans. "But did you have to spill it on *me?* You had the whole yard!"

Josh grinned. "Some people are never satisfied. I got you out of hot water, didn't I?"

"Right into cold lemonade," Ruth Rose said.

Dink blotted his jeans with a handful of paper napkins. "Come on. Let's go meet Mavis before my mom comes back. There's something weird happening on the third floor of the Shangri-la!"

Chapter 8

Dink's jeans were nearly dry by the time they reached the hotel. Mavis was waiting out front.

"How was your lunch?" she asked timidly.

"Fine, thanks," Dink said. "We talked it over, and we think there's something fishy going on on the third floor of this hotel."

Suddenly Mavis began coughing. She held up her scarf in front of her mouth.

Dink noticed that the letters on the

scarf were tiny M's. "Are you okay?" he asked.

"Should I run in and get you some water?" asked Josh.

Mavis took off her glasses and shook her head. "No, I'm fine, thank you. Dear me, I don't know what happened! Now, what were you saying about the third floor?"

"We think Wallis Wallace may be up there," Ruth Rose said. She reminded Mavis about the smudged signature for Room 302 and the Do Not Disturb sign on the door.

Mavis replaced her eyeglasses. "Mercy! What do you think we should do?"

"Follow me!" Dink said. For the second time, they all trooped into the hotel lobby.

Mr. Linkletter watched them from behind the counter.

"Hi," Dink said. "Remember us?"

"Vividly," Mr. Linkletter said.

"Wallis Wallace checked into Room 303, right?"

"That is correct," said Mr. Linkletter.

"Well, we talked to the maid who cleaned that room," Dink went on. "She told us no one slept in it."

"You spoke to Olivia Nugent? When? How?"

"We have our ways," Josh said.

"So," Dink went on, "we think Wallis Wallace disappeared right here in this hotel."

"And Wallis Wallace is a *very* famous writer," Ruth Rose reminded Mr. Linkletter. "Millions of kids are waiting to read his next book," she added sweetly.

Mr. Linkletter's sad eyes grew large. He swallowed and his Adam's apple bobbed up and down. He rubbed his forehead as though he had a headache.

Then Dink told Mr. Linkletter about Room 302. "Miss Nugent said there was a Do Not Disturb sign on the door."

Ruth Rose pointed to the register. "See? The signature is all smudged!"

"We think the kidnappers are hiding Wallis Wallace in that room!" Josh said.

At the word "kidnappers," Mr. Linkletter closed his eyes. He opened a drawer, took out a bottle of headache pills, and put one on his tongue.

"Just to be on the safe side, perhaps we should check both rooms, Mr. Linkletter," Mavis said quietly.

"It'll just take a minute," Dink said.

Mr. Linkletter let out a big sigh. "Very well, but this is most unusual. Things run very smoothly at the Shangrila."

They all got into the elevator. No one spoke. Dink watched Mr. Linkletter jiggling his bunch of keys. Mr. Linkletter kept his eyes on the little arrow telling them which floor they were on.

The elevator door opened on the third floor. Mr. Linkletter unlocked Room 303. "Most unusual," he muttered.

The room was empty and spotlessly clean. "Strange, very strange," Mr. Linkletter said.

They moved to Room 302, where a Do Not Disturb sign still hung on the doorknob.

Mr. Linkletter knocked. They all leaned toward the door.

"Listen, I hear a voice!" Josh said.

"What's it saying?" Ruth Rose asked.

Then they all heard it.

The voice was muffled, but it was definitely yelling, "HELP!"

Chapter 9

Mr. Linkletter unlocked the door and shoved it open.

A man with curly blond hair stared back at them. He was sitting in a chair with his feet tied in front of him. His arms were tied behind his back. A towel was wrapped around his mouth.

"Oh, my goodness!" Mr. Linkletter cried.

Everyone rushed into the room.

Dink ran behind the chair to untie the man's hands while Josh untied his

feet.

Mavis unwrapped the towel from around his face.

"Thank goodness you got here!" the man said. "I'm Wallis Wallace. Someone knocked on my door last night. A voice said he was from room service. When I opened the door, two men dragged me in here and tied me up."

He looked at Dink. "You're Dink Duncan! I recognize you from the picture you sent. How did you find me?"

"We followed your itinerary," Dink said. He showed Mr. Wallace the sheet of paper. "We got it from Mr. Paskey and used it as a trail. The trail led us to this room!"

"I'm so sorry I missed the book signing," Wallis Wallace said. "As you can see, I was a bit tied up."

He smiled. Then he rubbed his jaw. "My mouth is sore from that towel. I can't believe I was kidnapped! And I can't wait to get back to my safe little cottage in Maine."

"Can you describe the two guys who kidnapped you?" Dink asked. "We should tell Officer Fallon so he can try to find them."

Wallis Wallace stared at Dink. "The two guys? Oh...well, um, I don't think I'll—"

"HEY!" Ruth Rose suddenly yelled.

Everyone looked at her.

"What's the matter?" asked Dink. "You look funny, Ruth Rose."

Ruth Rose was staring at the red scarf draped around Mavis's neck. She pointed at the man who'd been tied up. "You're not Wallis Wallace!"

Then she looked at Mavis Green. "*You* are," she said quietly.

Chapter 10

"Ruth Rose, what are you talking about?" Josh said.

Dink didn't know what to think, except that he was getting a headache.

"What makes you think *I'm* Wallis Wallace?" Mavis asked.

Ruth Rose walked over to Mavis. "May I borrow your scarf?" she said.

Ruth Rose held the scarf up so everyone could see it. "When I first saw this scarf, I thought these little black letters were M's," she said. "M for Mavis."

She looked at Mavis Green. "But they're not M's, are they?"

She turned the scarf completely upside down. "What do they look like now?"

Dink stepped closer. "They're little W's now!"

"Right. Double-U, double-U for *Wallis Wallace!*" Ruth Rose pointed at the man. "You just said you live in a little cottage. But Wallis Wallace lives in a big *castle* in Maine. It says so on the cover of *The Silent Swamp.*"

Ruth Rose pointed at Mavis's book bag. "Seeing your bag again made me remember something I thought of today. Josh read that your castle was called Moose Manor. There's a picture of a moose on the side of your bag."

Ruth Rose handed the scarf back to Mavis. "And we read that Wallis Wallace's favorite color is green. You

like green ice cream, and you chose
Mavis Green for your fake name."

Everyone was staring at Ruth Rose,
except for the man they had untied. He
started laughing.

"The cat's out of the bag now, sis,"
he said.

Then Mavis laughed and gave Ruth
Rose a hug.

"Yes, Ruth Rose," Mavis said. "I really *am* Wallis Wallace." She put her hand
on the man's shoulder. "And this is my
brother, Walker Wallace. We've been
planning my 'kidnapping' for weeks!"

Dink stared at Mavis, or whoever
she was. "You mean Wallis Wallace is a
woman?" he said.

"Yes, Dink, I'm a woman, and I'm
definitely Wallis Wallace." She winked
at him. "Honest!"

Mavis, the real Wallis Wallace, sat on
the bed. She took off her glasses and

pulled the barrettes out of her hair. She shook her hair until it pulled out in a mass of wild curls.

"Thank goodness I can be myself now!" she said. "All day I've had to act like timid Mavis Green. I can't wait to get out of this fuddy-duddy dress and into my jeans again!"

She kicked off her shoes and wiggled her toes in the air. "Boy, does that feel good!"

Dink blinked and shook his head. Mavis Green was really Wallis Wallace? He couldn't believe it. "But why did you pretend to be kidnapped?" he asked.

The real Wallis Wallace grinned at the kids' surprised faces. "I owe you an explanation," she said.

"My new book is about a children's mystery writer who gets kidnapped. In my book, some children rescue the

writer. I wanted to find out how *real* kids might solve the mystery," she explained.

She smiled at Dink. "Then your letter came, inviting me to Green Lawn. That's what gave me the idea to fake my own kidnapping. I'd become Mavis Green and watch what happened."

"Oh, yeah!" Dink said. "In your let-

ter, you said you were doing some research in Connecticut."

She nodded. "Yes, and I mentioned the word 'kidnap' in the letter to get you thinking along those lines." She smiled at the three kids. "I thought I'd have to give you more clues, but you solved the mystery all by yourselves!"

Dink laughed. "You recognized me in

the bookstore from my picture," he said. "And you didn't send *me* a picture so I wouldn't recognize *you!*"

"Then my nutty sister dragged *me* into her plan," Walker Wallace said. "I should be home checking my lobster pots."

"While you were eating lunch, Walker and I ate ours up here," Wallis said. "Then, just before two o'clock, I tied him in the chair and ran downstairs to meet you out front as Mavis."

Wallis Wallace threw back her head and laughed. "Do you remember downstairs when Dink said there was something fishy on the third floor?"

She got up and stood next to her brother. "Well, I'm always teasing Walker about smelling fishy from handling his lobster bait. So when you said something was *fishy* in the hotel, I had to pretend to cough so you wouldn't

know I was really laughing!"

"Boy, did you have us fooled," Dink said.

Wallis Wallace grinned. "Mr. Paskey was in on it. I had to tell him the truth. As you saw this morning at the Book Nook, my little scheme made him very nervous. I've promised him I'll come back and do a real book signing soon. But I'll be in disguise, so be prepared for anything!"

Dink shook his head. "I was so disappointed because I couldn't meet my favorite author this morning," he said. "And I've been with you all day and didn't even know it!"

She looked at Dink. "I'm so sorry I tricked you. Will you forgive me?"

Dink blushed. "Sure."

"I have a question," Josh said. "Where did you really sleep last night?"

"Right here in Room 302. A few

weeks ago, I telephoned to reserve two rooms next to each other. Last night, I checked into Room 303 as Wallis Wallace, the man. Up in Room 303, I took off the hat and coat and sunglasses. Then I sneaked back down to the lobby wearing a blond wig. I checked in again, this time into Room 302."

"Did you smudge the signature?" Ruth Rose asked.

"Oh, you noticed that!" Wallis said. "I'm so used to signing my real name in books, I started to write *Wallis.* So I 'accidentally' smudged it."

"I have a question, Mavis, I mean Miss Wallace...what should we call you?" Dink asked.

"My friends call me Wallis," she said.

"Well, the taxi driver told us you were smiling in the taxi. What were you smiling about?"

Wallis Wallace was smiling now.

"Oh, about a lot of things. First, I was wearing a man's disguise, and that made me feel pretty silly. And I knew I was going to meet you, one of my biggest fans. And I was happy because I knew whatever happened, the next day would be fun!"

"I sure had fun," Josh said, grinning. "Poor Mr. Paskey, having to lie to everyone with a straight face!"

"Boy, did I have a hard time pretending to be Mavis all day," Wallis said. "But my plan worked. I met three brilliant detectives. You helped me to see how real kids would investigate a kidnapping. Now I can go back to Maine and finish my book."

"How come your book jackets never say that you're a woman?" Ruth Rose asked.

Wallis Wallace smiled. "Because of my name, most people assume that I'm a man," she explained. "I let them think that so I can do my research easier. I've learned that people clam up if they know I'm Wallis Wallace. So out in public I pretend I'm Mavis Green, just a regular person, not a mystery writer."

"I get it!" Dink said. "You don't have your picture on your books so people can't recognize you."

"Right. And I hope you'll keep my secret."

"We will. Right, guys?" Ruth Rose said.

"Thank you! Any more questions?" Wallis asked.

"Yeah," Walker said, giving his sister a look. "When do we leave? I've got lobsters waiting for me."

"I have a question, too," Dink said. "Will you send me your picture now?"

"Yes, but I'll do better than that," Wallis said. "I'll dedicate my next book

to my three new friends!"

Dink, Josh, and Ruth Rose did a triple high five.

"Excuse me," Mr. Linkletter said from the door where he had been standing.

They all looked at him.

"It's nearly checkout time."

Everyone laughed.

Mr. Linkletter smiled, but just a little.

A to Z Mysteries™

Dear Readers,

I still remember the day I decided to become a writer. On my tenth birthday, my parents gave me a copy of *King Arthur and the Knights of the Round Table*, and I couldn't put it down. Reading all those exciting adventures made me want to *write* exciting adventures!

I wrote stories all through high school and college. But I didn't think of writing for kids until years later, when I was teaching fourth grade. I was reading *Charlotte's Web* to my class when, suddenly, right in the middle of chapter three, a light bulb went off in my head: Why don't *you* write a children's book?

And I've been doing just that ever since.

I got the idea for *The Absent Author* a few years ago when I was invited to sign books at a small store in Vermont. The traffic was bad, and I arrived late.

One boy said, "Gee, Mr. Roy, I thought you'd been kidnapped or something!"

I thought about that all the way home. *The Absent Author* was born that day!

I had a great time writing *The Absent Author* and *The Bald Bandit*, the first two books in my new A to Z Mysteries series. I hope you have just as much fun reading them!

Sincerely,

Ron Roy

P.S. I love receiving mail, so feel free to drop me a line to tell me about yourself or just to say "Hi!" Please send your letters to:

Ron Roy
c/o Random House, Inc.
Maildrop 28-2
201 East 50th Street
New York, NY 10022

Collect clues with Dink, Josh, and Ruth Rose
in their next exciting adventure,

THE BALD BANDIT!

"Here's my plan," Dink said. "Every house we go to, we ask if anyone knows a skinny redheaded kid."

"That's *my* plan!" Ruth Rose said.

Dink grinned. "Oh, yeah, I forgot."

"We have to keep our eyes peeled," Ruth Rose continued. "Check out tall kids trick-or-treating."

"Got it," Dink said.

"Anyone with red hair, we ask them if they took a video of the bank robber," Ruth Rose went on.

"Check," Dink said. "Any other ideas?"

"Yeah, I got a great idea," Josh said. "Let's stop talking and get moving!"

I grab Louisa's arm and click off the flashlight she's holding. She's smart; she doesn't make a sound when she sees the look on my face, just before the light disappears. Behind us, Evelyn opens her mouth to ask one of her loud, yappy questions, but Louisa signals for quiet and Maddie claps her hand over Evelyn's mouth.

We stand very, very still.

There it is again.

Quiet, but unmistakable: out there in the dark, somebody hiccups. And it isn't one of us.

We're not alone.

Someone is following us through the forest.

TOMORROW GIRLS

TOMORROW GIRLS

GIRLS

Run for Cover

BY EVA GRAY

SCHOLASTIC INC.

New York   Toronto   London   Auckland
Sydney   Mexico City   New Delhi   Hong Kong

ISBN 978-0-545-31702-3

Copyright © 2011 by Tui T. Sutherland.
All rights reserved. Published by Scholastic Inc.
SCHOLASTIC and associated logos are trademarks and/or registered trademarks of Scholastic Inc.

12 11 10 9 8 7 6 5 4 3 2 1   11 12 13 14 15 16/0

Printed in the U.S.A.   40
First printing, July 2011

Designed by Yaffa Jaskoll

TOMORROW GIRLS

GIRLS

Run for Cover

Chapter 1

I'm not like the other girls.

Louisa and Maddie and Evelyn — it's like we're from totally different planets.

It's not just the obvious things, like the fact that I grew up with palm trees instead of pine trees, hibiscus instead of hydrangeas in my yard, tamales in place of tuna fish sandwiches for lunch.

It's not that I'm faster and stronger and better at surviving than they are . . . although I am.

It's not even that my home is gone, or that I watched it being swept away, while they have their nice comfortable houses to go back to, and they can't even imagine anything bad ever happening to them.

It's not all the secrets I'm hiding.

I'll tell you the biggest difference between us.

It's that they think they know what it's like to be scared.

But they have no idea.

We've been in the woods for only five minutes when I start thinking this escape might be a little bit doomed.

Not that we had any choice; we had to run away. Our parents sent us to a hidden boarding school because they wanted us to be safe from the dangers of the War. But it turned out we'd walked right into the worst danger of all.

Country Manor School did seem like a weird place from the beginning. They took away all our electronic devices, snipped off the ID bracelets we've been wearing our whole lives, and forced us to do our homework by hand. *By hand!* With *pens*! I should have *known* they were evil just from that!

But I figured they were just old-fashioned. Plus I liked the outdoor survival training and the friends I was making, and the chance to act like a regular girl again. If I'd been rooming with cooler people, I'd have been happier than I have been anytime in the last three years.

Then everything fell apart. First Louisa's "twin," Maddie, got caught. The headmistress, Mrs. Brewster, figured out that they weren't really sisters (something I could have told her on day two). Then Louisa overheard a TV news broadcast saying Canada had surrendered to the Alliance . . . who, in case you haven't guessed, are the bad guys in the War.

Canada's only a few miles from CMS, but that's not the dangerous part. The really bad news — the news that has us fleeing through the forest in the middle of the night — is that CMS is a sleeper cell and all our teachers are Alliance agents. The children of America's wealthiest families were brought here to be hostages. Louisa over-heard their plans, and we decided none of us were going to hang around and let Mrs. Brewster use us to manipu-late our parents.

So here we are: escaping, in the dark, with no idea how we'll get back to Chicago. And instead of any of my tough, cool, outdoorsy friends, I'm stuck with my suite mates.

I glance over at pale, blond Louisa. She can be cool sometimes. But the others, Maddie and Evelyn, are not exactly the first two people I would have picked to run away with. In fact, they're pretty much the last people anyone would want to drag through the woods. Maddie — skinny, brunette, brown eyes, looks nothing like Louisa, in case you're wondering — is always moping and griping; plus she totally hates me for no apparent reason.

And Evelyn is a world-class conspiracy freak, con-vinced that everyone is part of a secret Alliance plan. She's hyperalert all the time and she scribbles notes in her little notebook every time anyone says anything. Sure, okay, she's right some of the time, it turns out. But she is also annoying *all* of the time. And PS she hates me, too. Just because I made my own friends instead of sitting with my roommates at meals.

See why I'm a little worried about this escape plan? I'm not sure which is more likely: us getting captured by the Alliance, or Maddie and Evelyn throwing me under a bus the first chance they get. Or me losing my mind. That one could definitely happen, like, by the end of the night.

Maddie starts complaining first. "I'm tired," she says. "My feet hurt. Can we stop and rest?" She leans one hand against a tree and rubs her left ankle. There's a chilly breeze rippling through the leaves, which makes me nervous. It's only September, but we're so far north that it could get horribly cold very quickly — long before we reach Chicago, for instance. I'm not a big fan of the cold. Especially when I know I'll be sleeping outside for the foreseeable future.

"We've barely been walking for five minutes!" I say. Although we're surrounded by dark forest, we can still see the glow of lights from the school behind us. That means we're way too close, since the only lights still on are in the teachers' rooms. We need to get much, much farther away before we even think about stopping. I cross my arms and frown at Maddie.

"Yeah, but we hiked all weekend," Maddie points out, "and I'm still exhausted from that."

"Shhhh," Evelyn says. "They might have bugged the trees." Her dark skin blends into the shadows, but in the glimmers of moonlight I can see her eyes darting around in that annoying everybody's-after-us way that drives me crazy.

"Bugged the *trees*?" Louisa says. "That's a little paranoid, even for you."

Evelyn flares up at once. "I might be paranoid, but I'm right, aren't I? I mean, I was right about the school!"

I roll my eyes. "Maybe one or two of your insane theories were right, but when you're shooting a million ideas into the sky, it's not surprising that a couple of them will land."

"I was right that it was a conspiracy!" Evelyn's voice is getting too loud. "The Alliance *was* luring us into a trap! The secret locations, the weird classes, taking away all our electronics — it was all part of their plan!"

"Shhh, all right," Louisa says. "We're not disagreeing with you. You were right all along. You're a conspiracy-detecting genius. Is that what you want to hear?"

"Can we keep moving, please?" I say. Maddie sighs loudly, but she doesn't argue as we start walking again. I would rather try to find our way in the dark, letting our eyes adjust, but not enough moonlight penetrates the thick canopy of branches, so we have to use a flashlight. I let Louisa hold it, since she has a steady hand. Twigs and pine needles crackle and snap under our feet, and we're surrounded by the Christmas smell of the pine forest. If our situation weren't so utterly terrifying, it would be kind of nice and peaceful out here.

"I don't understand their plan, though, Evelyn," Maddie says after a minute. "If they were planning to hold us hostage for our parents' money, why would they teach us survival skills and all that other stuff? Why train us like we're soldiers? We'd never fight for the Alliance, no matter what they did to brainwash us!"

"Too right," I say. "I'd break Mrs. Brewster's face before I ever helped the Alliance."

"Wow, Rosie," Louisa says. "Tell us how you really feel. No, I'm kidding. I agree with you." A low-hanging branch snags her blond hair and she stops to disentangle herself.

"Maybe —" Evelyn says, and then pauses. Her shoulders are hunched and her hands are shoved in her jeans pockets.

"Maybe what?" I say.

"Never mind," she mumbles. "You'll just think it's stupid."

"I won't," Maddie says, bumping her shoulder. "Go ahead and tell us. I like hearing your theories."

I exchange a glance with Louisa. In the dark I can't see her expression, but I'm sure she's thinking what I am — that it's kind of annoying how Evelyn and Maddie always stick together and encourage each other's worst impulses. I don't say anything, though. As long as we're still walking, leaving CMS behind us, I don't care how much talking everyone else needs to do at the same time. If I were them, I'd be saving my energy, but I can only boss them around so much without someone snapping. I need to pick my battles.

"Well," Evelyn says, "I was just thinking . . . maybe not all the girls there were hostages. Maybe some of them were really on the Alliance's side." She hurries on before we can respond. "I mean, we don't really know anything about them. Maybe a lot of the others were being trained to fight in the War, and they knew it was secretly an Alliance training camp the whole time."

"I did hear something like that," Louisa says slowly. "The teachers were talking about getting certain girls to the cafeteria for a debriefing or something. The kids of Alliance parents."

We all fall silent. I think about my friends at CMS — Mary Jensen and Chui-lian Lee especially. I miss them. They would be a lot more useful out here than Evelyn and Maddie — that's for sure. I'd also take Anne or Erica or Rae or Carole over them any day. But were they all lying to me? Were they secretly working for the Alliance? Would they have turned on me and helped to hold me hostage if — when — everything came out in the open?

"I don't believe it," I say, but my voice catches, and I don't sound as confident as I want to.

Of course, part of me can't help wondering . . . if it's true, is the secret I'm keeping any better than theirs?

An hour later, I let everyone stop for a break. I'm a little worried about how deep in the forest we are. Evelyn is doing a great job with the compass, but I hope we can find a road to follow soon, at least from a distance. At the speed Maddie's going, I'm not sure staying in the woods will get us all the way back to Chicago anytime before January.

I crouch in a dim circle of moonlight under a break in the trees, stretching my aching muscles. I'd never admit this to the others, but I'm pretty sore after our long week-end of hiking, too. Part of me wishes we could have stayed at CMS for one more night, just to get a real night's sleep in a bed. But by tomorrow it would have been too late. Tonight was our only chance of escape.

"I wish we had our ID bracelets," Louisa says, rubbing her left wrist. "Maybe we should have tried to find them and steal them back. How are we going to get anywhere without them? How will we convince anyone we are who we say we are?"

"It's like they took my whole identity, not just a band of metal," Evelyn says. She's perched on top of a boulder. I'm sure she remembers my advice about not sitting down in case her muscles cramp, but if she doesn't care, I'm not going to keep bugging her about it.

"I know," Maddie agrees, climbing up next to her. "I feel naked without mine, especially now that we're away from the school."

I concentrate on my shoelaces. They don't know this, but their ID bracelets will be a lot easier to replace than

11

mine. I tried to act like I totally didn't care when Devi cut it off on the first day, but inside I felt like she might as well be cutting off my hands. Mom and Dad are going to be so unhappy with me when they find out it's gone. I wonder how much a new one will cost us this time, and whether we can use the same guy as before.

"I still don't understand why they took them," Maddie says with a sigh.

"To demoralize us," Evelyn says firmly. "It's classic psychological warfare. Take away our very identities, so we lose our senses of self and become easier to manipulate."

I can't help snorting. They all look over at me.

"You have a better theory?" Evelyn asks.

I hesitate. How much will I give away if I answer truthfully? Will they suspect anything?

Or will it be more suspicious if I don't answer at all?

"They're selling them," I say, rubbing my hamstrings and trying to sound casual. "A recoded ID bracelet is more valuable than a fake passport these days. The

Alliance uses them to get their agents in and out of the country without being caught."

Louisa gapes at me. "They can do that? Change all the information on the tag?"

"You know that," I say, nodding at Madeleine. "Didn't your family get someone to change her tag, so it said you were sisters?"

I hear Maddie's little intake of breath in the dark. "You told her we're not sisters?" she whispers.

"She figured it out," Louisa says. "And yeah, we did get a guy to do that, but all he had to change was her last name and her birthday. And I guess he didn't even do that right, since a ghost of her real info showed up on the tag when Mrs. Brewster scanned it."

I shake my head. "That probably only surfaced because they were trying to reformat and change the whole ID. Most hackers are better at it than your guy. Sorry." I shrug. "But they can construct entire new identities for people using an old bracelet bought on the black market."

I should know.

"Crazy," Evelyn says. "I bet they can raise a lot of money for the Alliance by selling them, too."

Louisa shivers. "I really hate the idea that some bad guy is out there wearing my ID bracelet, using it to sneak around and do horrible things."

I want to tell them that it's not only bad guys who need the black-market ID bracelets, but that would definitely give too much away. Safer just to change the subject.

"Sorry, everyone, but we should keep walking," I say. "Get as far as we can while it's still dark. Okay, Maddie? I know you can do it. You were totally tough on the camping trip." This is not entirely true; mostly she whined and grumbled a lot. But I'm sure she can be tougher with the right encouragement.

She sighs again, but she slides off the boulder and we all start walking through the trees in the direction Evelyn points, which I guess is still south. I try to stop worrying about how soon the Alliance will come after us, or how far we can get before morning, or what we're going to eat when we're hungry. I try not to think about how familiar this feels, the prickling sensation between my shoulder blades like someone is following us . . . someone who might suddenly shove a knife in my back at any moment.

I should feel calmer, out here where no one can see me. At least I'm not going to mess up and get caught by a teacher. No one's going to turn me in to the authorities. I don't have to freak out about following the rules anymore. I'm already so far outside the rules that now I just have to keep running until I get somewhere safe again.

But I won't feel comfortable until CMS is far, far behind us. If we get caught now, I could be in worse trouble than anyone else, even Maddie.

Night noises are all around us as we step cautiously through the trees, using only one flashlight to save batteries. I can hear crickets chirping and leaves rustling and a chorus of weird animal sounds, like snuffling and chittering and hiccupping and croaking . . .

Wait. Hiccupping?

15

I grab Louisa's arm and click off the flashlight she's holding. She's smart; she doesn't make a sound when she sees the look on my face, just before the light disappears. Behind us, Evelyn opens her mouth to ask one of her loud, yappy questions, but Louisa signals for quiet and Maddie claps her hand over Evelyn's mouth.

We stand very, very still.

There it is again.

Quiet, but unmistakable: out there in the dark, somebody hiccups. And it isn't one of us.

We're not alone.

Someone is following us through the forest.

Chapter 2

"Turn on your flashlight and keep walking," I whisper to Maddie. "Pretend you're still talking to me." Louder, I say, "Sorry, guys. I thought I heard something, but I guess I was wrong."

I tug Louisa behind a tree with me. Maddie switches on her flashlight and walks away with Evelyn close beside her. To her credit, she does a great job of pretending I'm still with them.

"Honestly, Rosie," she says, "you're starting to sound crazy like Evelyn."

"Hey!" Evelyn protests.

"I mean, you're making me totally nervous," Maddie goes on. "I'm sure nobody's even noticed we're gone yet, so we probably don't have to worry for a while. . . ." Her voice trails off into the woods as the little circle of light bobs away. I can feel Louisa tense; she doesn't love the dark settling around us, or watching her friends disappear up ahead. I fumble for her hand and squeeze it reassuringly. My heart is pounding, and I seriously wish we still had the rifles we used on the camping trip.

With the flashlight gone, my eyes start to adjust to the dark and the dim light from the moon, high above the trees. My ears feel like they're going to pop off my head, I'm listening so hard. Is that crack a branch being stepped on? Am I hearing someone's breathing, getting closer and closer?

Louisa sees it first, and she clutches my hand in a death grip.

A dark shadow moves out of the trees behind us and slowly edges past. Whoever it is, they're definitely following the sound of Maddie's voice, stepping lightly where our feet just were.

I crouch quietly and feel for a stick that's just the right size. My eyes scan the darkness, looking for more shadows. I spot another one a few feet away, flanking the one that's just gone by. I don't know if there are more of them out here in the woods. I have to decide whether to risk confronting them, or try sneaking away.

For a moment I think about how far Louisa and I could get on our own — how quickly we'd get back to Chicago, where we could warn our parents about what's happening. They could send help for Maddie and Evelyn. Nothing really bad will happen to them; I'm sure of it. The Alliance people at CMS would want Evelyn safe so they could get as much money as possible out of her parents.

But Maddie is nobody special; she wouldn't be valuable to them. Would they even keep her alive, now that she knows their secrets?

As much as I would like to, leaving the other two girls is not an option. I heft a stick in my hands and touch the end of it — perfect. I place Louisa's hand against the tree and pat it once: *stay here.* Then I creep out, one foot gently before the other, until I'm right behind the first shadow. His friend is ahead and to the left of us, so I can keep an eye on him, too.

I shove the end of the stick into the guy's back. "Stop right there."

He jumps a mile and tries to whirl around, but I've grabbed his arm to hold him in place, facing away from me. "Don't turn around," I say. "I don't know how much damage this rifle will do at such close range, but I bet you don't want to find out. Tell your friends to drop their weapons."

"W-w-we don't have any weapons!" he yelps. "I swear!"

I frown. His voice sounds familiar. And now that we're up close, I'm pretty sure he's only fourteen or fifteen, not much older than I am.

Louisa clicks on her flashlight, illuminating a head of short reddish-blond hair and a sage-green CMS T-shirt over stocky shoulders. The guy has his hands up in the air and keeps twisting his head around to try to see us.

"Ryan?" Louisa says from behind me.

"Louisa?" he says, nearly collapsing with relief.

I lower my fake rifle and let him go. Of course. Just my luck. It's those dingbat boys that Louisa dragged back to our campsite during our survival mission over the weekend — the ones from the boys' school across the lake. The boys who made the other girls so silly that they nearly ruined everything, just for the sake of a couple sandwiches and some flirting.

Nobody cared about what would happen to us if we got in trouble — how we might be sent home, or how the teachers might take a closer look at some of us who'd rather not attract any attention.

The other one comes crashing through the trees toward us. I catch a glimpse of his dark eyes and hair before he raises his hand to block the light. He's Hispanic, like me, and I wonder, not for the first time, where he's from.

21

I put my hands on my hips. "Good grief," I say, "are you guys *still* lost?"

"No!" says the light-haired one — Ryan. "We made it back to school, but then we were sent out again. This time we're supposed to survive out here for a week."

"A week!" Louisa says. "Why didn't they make us do that? That is totally sexist. Girls can survive in the wild just as well as boys."

"Yeah, especially if they happen to run into any boys carrying sandwiches," I point out.

I think she's about to yell at me, but then her face goes thoughtful and she turns back to Ryan. "*Do* you guys have any sandwiches?" she asks. "I mean, I assume you wouldn't say no to them this time, Queen Rosie? Now that we're *actually* trying to survive?"

The boys give her quizzical looks. Before I can answer her, we hear more branches snapping from up ahead of us, and then we see Maddie and Evelyn marching back through the trees. They're pushing a third boy along in front of them.

"Look what we found!" Evelyn says.

"He practically tripped over us," Maddie says. "Not very stealth." Her eyes widen as she spots the guys with us. "Wait — we know you! Ryan! Alonso!"

"Hey," says Alonso, giving Evelyn a friendly nod.

"This guy's with us," Ryan says, punching the new one in the shoulder. "His name is Drew. Drew, meet Louisa, Maddie, Evelyn, and Rosie." I have to admit I'm a little impressed he remembers our names, especially mine, since we didn't exactly meet in the friendliest way.

Drew is taller than the others, Asian American, good-looking, and wiry, with short, straight black hair. He's wearing a pair of sturdy silver-framed glasses and I spot a Swiss Army knife hanging from his belt. There's something about the way he stands and the way he looks at me that reminds me of Ivan — that same aura of secrets Ivan always had, like he knows more than I do.

Maybe it's unfair of me, but immediately I don't trust Drew. Even if he's just a regular guy, even if he would never do what Ivan did to my family, I don't want him around me. Or any of them, actually. Boys are an unwelcome — and dangerous — distraction.

"Are there any more of you?" I ask, scanning the trees. The wind seems to be picking up, and the branches are swaying over our heads so the shadows jump around in all directions. It's a little spooky.

Ryan shakes his head. He seems to be the unspoken leader of the guys, or at least the chattiest one. "It's a three-person mission," he says.

"With sandwiches?" Louisa asks longingly. He grins and nods at her.

"Why were you sneaking after us?" I demand.

"We were curious." Drew speaks for the first time. "We saw your light and wanted to know who else was out here." His voice is quiet and deep.

"Actually, we thought it might be Alliance spies," Alonso says. "Sneaking across the border from Canada and up to no good." He glances at Evelyn again; they both have the same bright-eyed, conspiracy-finding expression.

"We figured we'd get a medal or something if we caught you," Ryan adds with a grin.

I know he's joking, but his words send a bolt of alarm through me. What if they do decide to turn us in, or tell their teachers they saw us in the woods? I shiver, and it's not just from the cold breeze that's starting to whip our hair around.

"What about you?" Drew asks. "Why are you out here?"

"Just hiking," I say quickly, but, of course, at the same time Evelyn opens her big mouth and cries: "We're escaping!"

The boys all look startled. Ryan raises his eyebrows at Louisa, and Alonso's face lights up, but Drew looks straight at me, as if he can tell I'm hiding something.

"Escaping from our camping group," I say, jabbing Evelyn in the ribs. "They're so boring, yakking away about, uh —" I can't even think of anything believable. "Girl stuff. We needed a break, so we're taking a walk. That's all."

"Oh, come on, Rosie," Evelyn starts.

"But we should get back to them!" I say fast. I seize Evelyn's elbow in a way that I hope says, *Shut up shut up shut up now*. "Good luck with your survival mission. See you around." I try to pull Evelyn away, but she wrestles free of my grip.

"We should tell them the truth!" she insists.

"I think so, too," Louisa agrees. Some loyalty! I thought she trusted me to make decisions for the group. But I guess when it comes to boys, she can't even think straight. I should have learned that on our weekend trip when she sided with them over me. I glare at her.

"What do you mean?" Ryan says, looking from Louisa to me and back again. "What truth? What's going on?"

Louisa hesitates, glancing at me. To my surprise, it's Maddie who answers him. "It's not safe to stay at CMS," she says. "We heard something tonight. Well, Louisa did.

The school is an Alliance sleeper cell. They were going to use us as hostages to control our parents. Now that Canada has surrendered to the Alliance, we'd all be in danger if we didn't escape."

I notice that she doesn't mention what happened with her ID bracelet, or that Mrs. Brewster figured out she wasn't a Ballinger and put her in isolation. Even if Maddie trusts the boys more than I do, she still knows not to tell them all her secrets.

"Canada's fallen to the Alliance?" Ryan echoes. "Wow. That is — that is really not good." He crouches and runs his hands through his short hair, taking a couple of deep breaths.

"I knew it!" Alonso says. "I knew there was something weird about CMS! I told you!" He punches Drew in the arm and Drew rubs the spot, looking pained. For a moment I catch a glimmer on his face of the same frustration I feel whenever Evelyn is acting like a nut. Then it's gone, and he looks thoughtful again.

"Are you sure?" he asks us.

"I thought you liked CMS," Ryan says, standing up and turning to Louisa.

"I do! I mean, I did," she says. "That's why you have to believe me. I wouldn't say this if it wasn't true. I'm not —" She pauses, and I think she nearly said "crazy like Evelyn." "I'm not happy about it," she says instead. "I wanted CMS to be as great as I thought it was. But I know what I heard. If you're smart, you'll run away with us, too, for your parents' sakes."

"What?" My voice bursts out of my mouth before I can think. "Louisa! You can't just invite them along! We don't know these guys, we can't trust them, and we don't need them! We'd be better off on our own."

"I *do* know them," Louisa says hotly. "I know at least they wouldn't leave their roommates behind in the woods with no compass, like some people!"

"No, all you really know about them is that they'll give you sandwiches," I say. "But if that's all it takes to make you trust them more than you trust me, then maybe you should go with them and I'll find my own way back to Chicago. I bet I'd be safer that way anyhow!"

"Uh-oh," Evelyn interrupts, holding out her hands. A fat raindrop splatters on her palm. We all look up and realize that while we were arguing, the moonlight has been eaten by dark clouds, which have rolled in out of nowhere.

"Oh *no*!" Maddie yelps, and the skies open up.

Chapter 3

There's no way to keep arguing; the thunder drowns out our voices and the wind blows them away. It's one of those terrible storms that have gotten so much worse in the last twenty years, so every bit of rain is practically a hurricane. In moments, the storm is so strong that we can barely even stand under the deluge. I'm soaked to the skin and my backpack is a sodden weight on my back. I can hardly see the others in the dark and through the downpour.

I'm flipping through survival skills in my mind, trying to remember anything about what to do when a busload of rain is suddenly dumped on your head.

Lightning crackles above the trees and I think of flash floods and mudslides and worse. Suddenly I have the clearest memory of Wren's face, the way it changed when she saw the tidal wave coming. I hear her screaming at me to run all over again.

Panicking, I reach out blindly and grab the nearest person, thinking it's Louisa.

"Shelter!" I yell. "We have to find shelter!"

The person leans closer, touching my other arm, and I realize it's not Louisa, but Drew. I start to recoil, but he's pointing and waving something in his hand. I aim my flashlight at it and squint, realizing it's a compass. He pokes it with a finger and points again, off into the trees.

Someone blunders into us and clutches me with thin hands. Before I turn my flashlight on her, I can tell it's Maddie.

"We have to stay together!" I shout in her ear. I can't tell if she's heard me, but when I tug the gold cord out of my hair and twine it around my wrist and hers, she nods vigorously. A light flickers behind her and I see

31

Louisa and Alonso huddling close to us. I lift our linked hands and wave to Louisa to do the same.

Rain batters us relentlessly. It seems to take Louisa forever to work the elastic band out of her hair and loop it around her wrist and Maddie's. Alonso puts the flashlight between his teeth and reaches to help her.

I squint into the dark, searching for Evelyn and Ryan. Drew is still standing too close to me, holding the compass, waiting. I spot another weak circle of light and see Evelyn crouching beside a large boulder with her flashlight, trying to shield her backpack with her body. I point to her and Drew goes over to bring her back to us.

When I look around, blinking in the driving rain, Alonso has tied himself to Louisa's free hand and is working on wrapping something around his wrist and Ryan's. I guess we're stuck with the boys, at least for now.

Drew's hand slips into mine just as a peal of thunder rolls overhead, and I jump. He waves the compass and points again. I nod. I have no choice. If he knows where we can find shelter, we have to follow him, although every cell in my body is screaming not to trust him.

Evelyn joins the end of the line, holding Ryan's hand, although she's still clutching her backpack to her chest with her other hand. I want to tell her that whatever's in there isn't worth it — I guess she's worried about her maps — but there's no way she'll hear me through the screaming wind.

Mud sloshes over our shoes as we slog forward, heads down. The world shrinks down to Drew's warm hand on one side and Maddie's cold, thin hand on the other. The rest of me is wet through and through, freezing and soaked and heavy, so moving is difficult. We slip on waterlogged leaves, stumble through giant puddles. My feet have never been this cold before.

The most annoying part is my hair. Without the cord tying it back, the long dark strands whip mercilessly around my head, stick to my face, and nearly blind me. But I can't reach up to shove it back because both of my hands are occupied. I keep shaking my head, but all that does is plaster more long tendrils to my face.

Suddenly Maddie lets out a shriek and I feel her hand jerk away. There's a wrenching pain in my wrist as the gold cord tightens and my shoulder is nearly yanked out of its socket. I try to let go of Drew, but his grip on my hand is too strong.

"Maddie!" Louisa screams. We both lean over, grabbing for her hands. The ground below Maddie has turned into a river of mud, dropping out from under her so that she nearly slid away down a hill that wasn't there a moment ago. If we hadn't been tied together, she'd have vanished into the dark.

Without letting go of me, Drew helps us and Alonso drag Maddie back onto solid ground. She leans on Louisa's shoulder, and I'm pretty sure she's crying, although it's hard to tell in the rain. I pat her arm awkwardly, her hand hanging limply from the cord tying us together.

"Not much farther," Drew shouts in my ear. I don't

know where he could be taking us. Surely the only shelter nearby is back at CMS — our school or theirs. Is he going to turn us in? I can't help thinking of Evelyn's last theory, that maybe some of the students were really working for the Alliance all along. What if she's right, and what if Drew is one of them?

But there's not much I can do now except follow him.

The rain pours down on us, harder and harder, each droplet like an exploding ice bomb on my bare neck and hands, slithering down into my sleeves. I can't even figure out which direction we're going. Back toward CMS? South, like we were before? I'm totally discombobulated, and I hate it.

Drew stops suddenly and I crash into him. He reaches over with his free hand and pushes my hair out of my eyes, then gestures at a clearing up ahead of us. In a flash of lightning, I spot a dark shape that could be a small cabin.

Everyone moves faster as we cover the last stretch of muddy ground, energized by the sight of shelter. All at once there's a blue door right in front of us: wooden, solid, real. I notice that Drew doesn't knock. He tries the handle, and my heart sinks when I see that it's locked.

But then he crouches and starts picking up large rocks next to the door. I watch him, confused, until he finds a small cavity on the underside of one of them and pulls out a key.

How did he know that would be there?

He unlocks the door, and we all pile inside so fast you'd think it was tigers chasing us instead of a storm. I suck in a breath of dry air and lean against the nearest wall. A wave of exhaustion hits me hard.

The door clicks shut behind us. The howling noise of the storm is instantly muffled. Finally we can hear ourselves think again.

Unfortunately, that also means we can hear one another talk.

"I thought we were going to die," Maddie gasps. She doesn't help as Louisa and I untie the cords around our wrists. As soon as I'm done, she slides down the wall and rests her head on her knees, making little sniffly noises.

Part of me is irritated — she wasn't the only one out there, after all — but part of me realizes that she's never been outside in a storm like that before. I'm probably the only one here who's ever lived through a superhurricane. I glance at Alonso, wondering again if he might have a secret like mine.

A light flickers on overhead and we all turn to Drew, who's found a switch on the wall. We're standing in a kind of vestibule, a small space with an open archway ahead of us into a bigger room. We're all dripping onto a red terra-cotta tile floor. There are neat brass shoe racks on either side of us and a coatrack in the corner. I'm relieved to see that they're empty, although I could probably guess that we're the only people here by the dark rooms beyond the vestibule.

Where is *here, anyway?*

"What is this place?" I ask Drew.

He shrugs. "I'm not sure. I found it on one of my first

solo survival missions, a couple of weeks ago. There wasn't anyone here then, either."

I squint at him. "So how'd you know where the key was?"

His smile is a little condescending, like he thinks it's cute how suspicious I am. I wonder if he'd also find it cute if I punched that smile off his face.

"Lucky guess," he says. "My parents have a rock like that."

Liar, I think. Outside of CMS I don't know anyone who uses real keys anymore.

"I don't care what it is," Louisa says. She's already dumped her backpack on the floor and she's taking her shoes and socks off. "There must be towels here. That's all I want in the world. A dry towel. And some dry clothes. And maybe a hair dryer. And some food. Hot chocolate. And a bed with lots of pillows."

I can't help laughing. "But that's all, right?"

She smiles at me, and I remember why I like her. Nothing ever seems so bad to Louisa. I know that's just

38

because nothing bad has actually ever happened to her, but it's still kind of nice to be around someone who thinks everything will be okay, no matter what. She's like the opposite of my parents, who worry that something terrible is coming around every corner, and they're usually right.

"Whoa," Ryan says, peering into the next room. "Guys, check this out."

The others crowd around him, but I take a minute to put down my backpack, take off my shoes, and wring out my socks and my hooded sweatshirt. I wish I could take off more of my dripping-wet clothes, especially my jeans, but of course I can't, because of the stupid boys. If it were just me, Louisa, Maddie, and Evelyn, we wouldn't have to worry and I'd be able to get dry a lot faster.

By the time I join the others in the main central room of the cabin, which is up two small steps from the vestibule, Ryan has found another light switch and turned on the low-hanging lamp in the center of the room.

I guess I expected couches and a coffee table and a fireplace and maybe a moose head on the wall, like a regular cabin in the woods where people went to fish or whatever in the old days, before the War. Instead there's an enormous oval conference table taking up almost the entire room. The polished mahogany surface gleams in the lamplight. Dark blue swivel chairs are arranged neatly around the oval, with a sort of uncanny precision that gives me goose bumps. The light barely reaches the edges of the table, but under my feet I can feel a textured carpet like the one in my dad's office at home, solid and businesslike.

Creepiest of all, up on the large blank wall opposite us is the seal of the Alliance.

This is definitely not a fishing cabin.

And we are definitely, definitely not supposed to be here.

Evelyn's eyes are huge. "It's their secret Alliance meeting place," she whispers. "This must be where they come to plan their invasion — to meet up with the teachers from your side!" she says to Alonso.

"I bet you're right!" he says. "I bet after they send us all into the woods on our made-up missions, they come here and plan real ones."

My instinct is to scoff at them or crack a joke of some kind, but there's something about the freaky, quiet intensity of this room that makes it too easy to believe what they're saying. I can absolutely picture Mrs. Brewster sitting at one end of the table, calmly passing around file folders full of notes on all the CMS students . . . and discussing how much money they can probably get for each of us.

I wonder what their notes on me would say, and how much they know. Do they realize that my parents will pay anything to get me back, because they're so afraid to lose the only daughter they have left? Is there anything in the CMS files about my missing sister, or is Wren a secret from them, too?

"Well, it's not an ordinary cabin — that's for sure," Ryan says. "I mean, who can afford electricity for a random cabin in the woods these days? It must have its own generator and everything."

We all glance up at the light, and I shiver again.

Louisa's voice breaks the tension. "There's a bathroom back here," she says from a doorway in the far corner. "Not a lot of towels, though. Whatever they use this place for, I don't think sleeping or bathing is a big part of it." She comes out with an armful of lilac-colored hand towels. We each take one and I run mine along my arms, then rub my hair with it. It's not the most useful thing ever, but it's better than nothing.

I notice that Louisa gives Maddie two hand towels and then helps her dry her hair with one of them. I can see why most people would believe that they're sisters. That's something Wren would have done for me. It's only because I think about Wren all the time that I noticed the little ways Louisa and Maddie don't act like sisters.

Thinking about my family sends me on a search for a telephone, but of course there isn't one anywhere in the cabin, nor a computer or anything useful like that. The other door off the room leads to a tiny kitchen, although the fridge turns out to be woefully understocked. Everything in the cupboards has that NutriCorp logo on it, like the food in the CMS cafeteria. I pull out a box of oatmeal cookies and peek inside. Only half of them are gone.

"Hey, Louisa, guess what?" Ryan says. "I can make one of your dreams come true, at least." He waggles a packet of cocoa at her. She clasps her hands rapturously, looking like a cartoon-character version of happy.

"Wait," Evelyn says, closing the refrigerator door in Drew's face. "Stop! You guys, we shouldn't take anything. Or else they'll know we were here! We can't leave any traces!"

"Ohhh," Maddie says anxiously. "You're totally right. She's totally right! Guys, put everything back exactly where you found it! We should wipe down everything we touched!"

I roll my eyes. "They're not going to dust for fingerprints, Maddie."

"How do you know?" she demands.

"They don't even *have* our fingerprints to compare them to," I point out.

"Oh," she says. "Okay. True. But —"

"But I'm hungry!" Louisa says. "And the Alliance deserves to be stolen from!"

"Maybe they won't notice *one* cocoa packet," Ryan suggests. "Or two? Maybe a couple of cookies?"

"It doesn't matter," Drew says. "We should take whatever we want. They'll know we were here, anyway."

"How?" I ask. *Because you're going to tell them?*

He points down at the floor, then back at the rug behind us. "Even with our shoes off, we've really messed up the carpet. It won't take an enormous brain trust to figure out that someone sheltered in here from the storm."

He's right. There are wet patches and bits of grass and mud all across the pale blue carpet. The hem of my jeans is busily creating its own little mud puddle right here in the kitchen.

"They won't know for sure it was us," I say to Evelyn and Maddie. "They might think it was some of the boys on their survival mission."

"Hey, that's true," Ryan says. "Since they're not expecting me and Drew and Alonso back for a week, they won't even start looking for us until we don't show up."

There's an awkward pause. It takes Ryan a minute to figure out that's because I still haven't agreed to let them come with us, and he gives me an apologetic look.

"Listen, we can't go back to CMS after what you guys told us," he says. "We don't want to be used as weapons against our parents any more than you do. If you won't let us come with you, we'll have to run away on our own."

This sounds like a fine plan to me, but Louisa immediately jumps in. "Don't be silly," she says. "We want you with us. We'll be safer if we stick together."

45

That is blatantly false, but I'm guessing she doesn't want to hear about how a large group will make more noise crashing through the woods, or how much easier it'll be to spot all of us from their helicopters, or how much harder it'll be to find somewhere for us all to sleep safely, never mind finding food for seven instead of four. Safer! We might as well turn ourselves in right now.

"Right, Rosie?" Louisa says. "I mean, look at these poor, helpless guys. They obviously need us."

Ryan tries to make puppy-dog eyes. Alonso's friendly, harmless expression is more successful. Drew, on the other hand, still has that I-know-things face, and he raises his eyebrows at me as if he's curious to see what I'll do, not that it actually matters to him one way or another.

It occurs to me that if he is working for the Alliance, maybe I *should* keep him with us, so I can keep an eye on him.

"Fine," I say, pulling my hair back into a ponytail and wringing it out. "You're right. If we didn't let them come with us, they'd probably end up wandering in circles around the school until they got caught."

"We would," Ryan agrees affably. "We'd be lost without you."

"I'm not as bad as these two," Drew offers. "*I* can actually start a fire, for instance."

"So can I!" Alonso protests. He leans over to the stove and flicks one of the knobs. Blue light flares around one of the burners. "See? I rock at this."

Louisa and Maddie both giggle. Oh, brother. I bet there's going to be a lot of that — laughing at stupid boy jokes that aren't even that funny. I reach over and turn the knob off. We have our own generator at home, too, but I still hate wasting energy.

"So, hot cocoa for everyone?" Louisa says hopefully.

I go back out into the vestibule while the others search the kitchen for mugs. There's a small window by the front door that's covered with a close-fitting dark shade, I guess so no one will see the cabin's lights from the woods. I peek out just in time to see a huge flash of lightning. This storm isn't stopping any-time soon.

"We'll have to sleep here tonight," Drew says from right behind me, peering over my shoulder at the rain.

I whirl around and shove him back. "*Don't* sneak up on me."

"I didn't mean to," he says, raising his hands, palms out. "I came to get the sleeping bags, to see if they'd dry out if I unroll them."

"Me, too," I say. There's only one thing I like about Drew so far, and it's that he seems to have a sensible head on his shoulders. He keeps doing the same things I would do to survive. The problem is, I don't trust his reasons. Maybe he was going to use the sleeping bag idea as an excuse to go through our packs. Or maybe he has a hidden Alliance communicator in his.

I watch him carefully as we both unpack the sleeping bags and shake them out, but I don't catch him sneaking anything out of his pack, or any of the others. We spread the sleeping bags around the giant conference table, head to toe, although there's not quite enough room and one of them has to go under the table, between the chairs.

Despite the drenching downpour, the sleeping bags were pretty well protected in their waterproof bags, and are mostly dry. I wish I could say the same for the clothes in our packs, but they're a little drier than the ones I'm wearing, so I slip into the bathroom and change into new jeans and a warm, long-sleeved black shirt.

When I come back out, Louisa has just emerged from the kitchen with two mugs of cocoa. She sets them down on the table with a flourish. "Maybe they'll stain the wood," she says. "It would serve them right."

"Yeah," I say. "Take that, Alliance! That'll teach them for defeating Canada and kidnapping us!"

Louisa giggles again. To her disappointment, though, the mugs don't leave any marks on the table. They're a plain, institutional white porcelain with the NutriCorp logo emblazoned on the side. I have to look at it twice before I realize it's not the Alliance seal, though. From a distance, and when I'm this tired, the logo and the seal look eerily similar, except that the logo has a maple leaf where the Alliance seal has a giant star.

I barely have the energy to drink my cocoa, although it does warm me up and make me feel a bit better. I have no idea how far we've come from CMS, although I'm very sure it's not far enough. But at least we're safe from the storm, and we can get some sleep before moving on. Hopefully it'll have stopped raining by morning. We're getting out of here as soon as it's light, storm or no storm.

I crawl into the sleeping bag under the table. Louisa, Ryan, Maddie, Alonso, and Evelyn stay up for a while longer, talking. I can hear them giggling as I drift off to sleep. It makes me feel a little left out and a lot grumpy, even though I don't want to join them. Only Drew is sensible enough to also get the rest we all need.

But I'm not going to go out there and yell at them. The girls know perfectly well how I feel about getting distracted by boys, I think. It won't be my fault when they're tired tomorrow.

Something is digging into my back, but I'm too tired to wriggle away from it. I close my eyes and dream, as I always do, of hurricanes and tidal waves, of Wren smiling up at Ivan, of swimming and running and hiding and helicopters, of the look on my mom's face as a new ID bracelet is snapped around my wrist. Only this time, Ivan has Drew's face, and when I look up from my ID bracelet, the person putting it on me, smiling evilly, is Mrs. Brewster.

I can even hear her loud, brassy voice. It's so real. . . .

I jolt awake, all the hairs on my skin standing on end.

It *is* real.

Mrs. Brewster is *here*.

Chapter 4

Runaways," Mrs. Brewster snaps. I'm so befuddled and sleepy and out of it that it takes me another twenty seconds to realize her voice is coming from outside the cabin, not right above me like I first thought. I sit up fast and bang my shoulder on one of the rolling chairs, just barely missing the table with my skull.

"Louisa!" I hiss quietly. I duck my head to look under the chairs and I see Louisa's wide, frightened blue eyes peeking out of her sleeping bag. She hears our headmistress, too.

"Four of them!" Mrs. Brewster goes on. The storm has passed, or else we wouldn't be able to hear her so clearly. If it had still been raining, she would have walked in and found us asleep. "Just when things were going so perfectly! Where could those idiot girls have gone?"

I wince. She's talking about us! Of course, those "idiot girls" are nanoseconds away from being back in her clutches. There's nowhere for us to hide, no way to run before she walks through the door. My heart is pounding and I can barely breathe. What will happen to my family now?

"What is taking so long?" Mrs. Brewster barks.

"I can't find the key," says Devi's voice. "It's like someone moved all the rocks around."

"Connolly," Mrs. Brewster snorts. "He has no discipline."

I scramble out from under the table and nearly crash into Drew's legs. He meets my eyes and holds up the cabin door key, but his face is pale, and for the first time he looks really worried. He never put it back last night, so we're safe for another minute, but not much more.

53

"Is there another way out of here?" I whisper.

On the other side of the table, Louisa shakes Maddie awake and then Evelyn, covering Evelyn's mouth as she opens her eyes to make sure Evelyn doesn't start yakking and give us away. Alonso climbs blearily out of his sleeping bag and pokes Ryan with his toe.

"I don't know," Drew whispers back. "Not that I know of, but I've never, like, hung out here."

"Get our stuff from the vestibule," I say to Louisa and Evelyn. "All of it! Don't leave anything behind. Put your shoes on and roll up the sleeping bags." I don't have time to act like we're all a happy decision-making team right now. I can't believe we're such morons! Of course the teachers would show up here first thing in the morning, ready to discuss their new plans now that Canada has fallen. We could not have picked a worse place to hide.

This turns out to be truer than I first thought as I search for another exit. The bathroom window is way too small for any of us to fit through, except maybe Maddie.

54

Outside I can see the grayish-blue-pink light of early dawn; it's maybe five in the morning or something horrible like that.

The kitchen doesn't even have any windows, and neither does the conference room. There's no back door. There's only the front door, where Mrs. Brewster is standing, clearly getting more and more impatient. I tug on my socks and shoes as quietly as I can, listening through the wood.

"I'm sorry, Mrs. B.," Devi says. "I found the rock, but the key isn't in there. Someone must have taken it with them last time."

"Idiots," Mrs. Brewster growls. My hopes rise a tiny bit. Maybe they'll have to go away and get a new one, and we can escape while they're gone.

"Connolly and Grifone will be here soon," Devi says. "One of them probably has it."

"I'm not standing here waiting for them like an abandoned dog," Mrs. Brewster says. "Run back to the truck and get our extra key."

55

"Yes, boss," says Devi.

I dash back into the main room. The others are huddled around the table, looking terrified. "We have maybe a minute," I whisper. "Then it's all over." I press my hands to my forehead, trying to think. There must be something we can do. We can't have failed so quickly, so spectacularly. This has to be the worst escape in the history of the world.

And it's Drew's fault, I think, suspicion bubbling up inside me. But the truth is, if I had known about this place, I probably would have brought us here in the storm, too.

"There are seven of us," Ryan points out. "I hate to say it, but I bet we could overpower her if we try to make a run for it right now."

"Have you seen her?" Maddie asks with a shudder. "She could take all of us down easily."

"Plus she probably has a weapon," Evelyn whispers. "Most likely secret, advanced Alliance technology."

This is such an Evelyn thing to say that Louisa can't help rolling her eyes at me, despite how tense the situation is.

"And even if a few of us get away, she's bound to catch someone," says Alonso, keeping his voice low like the rest of us. "And she'll know exactly how far the rest of us have gone, so we'll all be in cells by the end of the day."

I have no idea what to suggest. My sleeping bag is poking out from under the table, so I crouch down to drag it out while the others argue. I'm a little annoyed no one has packed it up for me while I was searching for an escape route.

The zipper catches on something, and I have to lean in to unhook it. When I see what it's hooked on, I nearly yell with excitement, but I manage to keep my voice down.

"Guys!" I hiss, poking my head out. "There's a trapdoor under the table!"

Drew and Louisa shove chairs aside and duck under with me. Together we turn the silver metal handle in the floor until there's a click and we can heave the trapdoor up.

I shine my flashlight down the dark hole and we see a dirt floor about eight feet below us.

"This doesn't seem like a good idea," Maddie says.

"All we've got left are bad ideas," I say. I scoot my feet over the edge, drop my backpack and sleeping bag down ahead of me, and jump after them. Quickly I spin with the flashlight, thinking it's a cellar of some kind, and maybe we can hide in it until the Alliance meeting is over.

I catch my breath. Even better. "There's a tunnel down here! We can get out this way!"

"But where does it go?" Maddie frets.

"Away from Mrs. Brewster," Louisa says. "That's all I need to know." She drops her backpack down next to me and swings herself through the hole as well. "Come on, Maddie!"

"Hurry!" I add.

"Maybe Ryan, Alonso, and I should stay here," Drew suggests, to my surprise, as Maddie reluctantly lowers herself through the hole. His face peers down at us, hidden by the shadow of the table above him. "That way if they figure out someone was here, we can pretend we just got lost during the storm. It'll draw attention away from you girls."

Louisa reaches out and catches Maddie as she stumbles away from the hole. Evelyn drops down right behind her. I see the expression on Louisa's face: she knows Drew has made a good suggestion, but she's still reluctant to leave the boys.

It's the perfect chance for me to get rid of them . . . but I can't. I know what's likely to happen to them if they stay. Even if Mrs. Brewster believes their story — which she won't — they'll never have a chance to run away after this. And what if Alonso does have a secret like mine? Then he really can't afford to get caught, either.

59

"That won't work," I call up to Drew. "There are seven used mugs of cocoa. They'll know you were with us. Quick, rearrange the room like it was as much as you can, then get down here."

Beside me in the dim light, Evelyn smacks her forehead. "I guess my mom was right about doing the dishes as soon as you've used them."

"We're so dumb," Louisa mutters anxiously.

"We can still get out of this," I say. "If they don't figure out we've used the trapdoor, hopefully they'll think we're in the woods nearby and they'll go out looking for us."

There's a thump as Ryan lands behind us, followed by Alonso. Drew jumps down last, and then Ryan lifts him on his shoulders so that Drew can reach the trapdoor and close it. Just as he turns the knob to lock it, we hear footsteps marching across the floor above us.

We all freeze, holding our breath.

"Of course Connolly is late, as always," Mrs. Brewster grumbles over our heads. "Devi, did you bring the folders on those four girls?"

"Of course," Devi answers. "And their ID bracelets. The data history might tell us something about where they're going, if we can retrieve it."

"I wonder if any of the boys are missing, too," says the headmistress.

"I'm sure not. None of the hostages know about what's happened in Canada," Devi says reassuringly. "It's bad timing — that's all. The Ballinger girl was worried about her fake sister. That's why they ran away, so they wouldn't get in trouble. They don't know about us."

"I hope you're right," Mrs. Brewster muses. "But it's a strange coincidence, on the very day we're able to reveal our true purpose. And why would Posner and Chavez go with them? Blast it all. I knew those girls were trouble from the beginning. I should have locked all four of them up on day one."

I wave my hand to get everyone's attention. Fascinating as this is, it can't be long before Mrs. Brewster notices something — the mud on the carpet, or the mugs in the sink, or the extra hand towels draped around the bathroom. We've done a terrible job of covering our tracks. And we need to run. Now.

We don't risk talking or even whispering. Ryan sets Drew down carefully and I head for the tunnel. My flashlight reveals nothing but packed dirt walls all around us. There's no way to know what's up ahead.

But whatever it is, it's got to be better than being dragged back to CMS by Mrs. Brewster so our parents can spend all of their money trying to get us home.

I take a deep breath. And then I lead the way into the darkness.

Chapter 5

It is surprisingly cold in the tunnel, especially since my clothes aren't completely dry yet. My feet squish in my sneakers and my jeans feel clammy against my thighs. I wish I could stop and at least put on a pair of dry socks, but as long as we're moving, I'm not going to be the one to slow us down. Our close call back at the cabin seems to have lit a fire under Maddie and Evelyn, and neither of them so much as peeps a complaint even after two hours of walking.

A drumbeat of worry keeps going around and around in my head. Where is the tunnel taking us? What if they figured out we went this way and are waiting for us at the other end? Drew was the last one through the trapdoor — what if he left a message for them to come get us? I don't see any branches off this tunnel. It goes one way, and one way only. If anyone comes along the tunnel, from either direction, we're as trapped as we were in the cabin.

Not to mention how unexcited I am about finding out where an Alliance tunnel could possibly lead. I'm guessing it won't be Chicago.

After a while, Evelyn pulls out her compass. She flicks on her flashlight — again, we're using only one, to save batteries — checks the needle, and grimaces.

"What?" Alonso asks.

"That's what I was afraid of," she says. "So much for heading south to Chicago."

"Why? What direction are we going in?" asks Louisa.

Evelyn holds out the compass to her. "Due north."

Louisa looks down at it, biting her lip. I know she's thinking the same thing I am. Due north means

Canada. Only a few short miles away. Which has just fallen to the Alliance. We've been walking for such a long time, we might even have crossed the border already.

"What are we going to do if we end up in Canada?" Maddie says, wide-eyed. "Without our ID bracelets, we'll be in such huge trouble."

"Even *with* them we'd be in trouble," Evelyn says.

"That's true," I say. "Now that Canada's on the other side of this war, it's going to be ten thousand times as hard to cross the border and get home again." I know way, way too much about that. I doubt any of my six companions could survive a clandestine border-crossing run.

"Maybe we should go back to the cabin," Ryan says, slowing down and looking back over his shoulder. "Maybe they'll be gone by now."

"That'd be better than getting stuck in Canada," Alonso says. "Most likely in a war zone."

"Unless we run into our teachers coming this way,"

Drew says grimly. "We can't go back. We have to go forward."

I hate agreeing with him, but I do. In this case, the unknown is a much preferable alternative to what we know is back there. At worst, surely we can find a phone somewhere in Canada and call our parents. I want them to know that we're out of Mrs. Brewster's clutches. And once they know where we are, maybe they can come get us.

But as I think about that for the next half hour of walking, I begin to wonder if it's true. Maybe Ryan's plan would be better. My parents certainly wouldn't have an easy time coming to get me from Canada. What if we step out right into a war zone, as Alonso said? What if the Alliance catches us right away? Or what if we get to the border, but there's no way to get across and get home?

I'm about to suggest turning back when, all of a sudden, the tunnel ends.

Maddie's flashlight beam hits a packed dirt wall ahead of us. Dirt walls on either side. We've reached the end, wherever this is.

Maddie just stands there for a moment, staring at the wall in confusion, so I take the flashlight from her and point it up at the ceiling.

A couple of metal rungs are driven into the side of the wall, leading up to another trapdoor, with the same kind of silver metal lock as the one in the cabin. We all gaze up at the new trapdoor, and I'm pretty sure it's safe to say we're all terrified.

"They could be waiting for us," Evelyn points out. "There could be motion detectors in this tunnel that let them know we were coming. Or security cameras!"

Trust Evelyn to make a spooky situation even worse.

"We haven't seen anything like that," I say, trying to sound reassuring.

"The Alliance wouldn't need to put special defenses on their top secret tunnel," Louisa agrees. She combs her blond hair back with her fingers and twists it into a braid like she's getting ready to run.

"Not at this end, anyway," Alonso offers.

Louisa and Maddie both nod like he's said something terribly smart, but the only one he's looking at is Evelyn. She bites her fingernails, blinking at the trapdoor.

"Well, it's forward or back," says Ryan. "I say let's see where we are."

He takes a step toward the rungs, and although I appreciate his boldness, I can't stand letting a guy be the bravest one in our group.

"I'll do it," I say, jumping in front of him. I drop my backpack, grab the handholds, and clamber up the couple of feet to reach the trapdoor. The lock sticks for a moment, and it's especially hard with just one hand, but I throw all my weight at it and finally it slides aside with a *clunk*.

Cautiously, I lift the trapdoor half an inch and peek out.

The morning light is bright enough that my eyes, used to the dimness of the tunnel, take a minute to adjust.

So the first thing I know is that we're outdoors, not coming up into another cabin.

As soon as I can see, my eyes land on a stack of white boxes, all of them with the NutriCorp label on the side. They look like they've been piled up on the grass, waiting to be taken somewhere. Maybe into the tunnel? So they can be smuggled to CMS? But it seems like a lot of boxes. I wonder if there are that many people planning to carry them all the way back down the long tunnel we just came through.

I try craning around, squinting through the small gap between the trapdoor and the ground. Now I can see small wooden buildings and canvas tents, kind of like a summer camp from old movies, back when kids had fun in the summertime, swimming and doing talent shows or whatever. But instead of kids in swimsuits, the people striding around here are all adults . . . and they're all wearing military uniforms and boots.

Alliance military uniforms.

And fluttering above the camp is a giant flag with the Alliance seal on it. They wouldn't dare fly that so openly in the United States.

So I can be pretty sure our worst fear is true: we've crossed the border into Canada, and landed smack in the middle of an Alliance military camp.

Chapter 6

I whisper the bad news down to the others. Maddie lets out a little moan and sits down on the dirt floor, leaning against Louisa's leg. But Evelyn and Alonso actually look excited.

"Maybe we can find something to help the Resistance," Evelyn says.

"The what?" Ryan asks.

She rolls her eyes at him. "Don't you pay attention to the news? The Resistance is fighting the Alliance wherever the military can't. They're exactly the people we need to take down the sleeper cells and training camps. If we could get a message to them, they'd rescue all the girls at CMS."

"Are you serious?" Drew says, pushing his glasses up on his nose. "I thought the Resistance was an urban legend. Where do you get your 'news'?"

Evelyn flushes. "The Internet. And maybe some message boards."

"Oh, message boards," Drew says. "I see. Very reliable."

"Hey, I've heard of the Resistance, too," Alonso says, touching Evelyn's elbow. "I think they're real. *Somebody* put out that fire in Baltimore. They disabled those bombs in Cleveland. They saved that evacuation train full of people when it ran out of fuel in the middle of Missouri. They've been ferrying supplies to the people who are still trying to live in California with no electricity. And I've heard they help refugees get into the country when their own homes get too dangerous." I flinch, remembering kind green eyes behind a makeshift mask and their sad expression when I asked about Wren. "If it's not the Resistance, who's doing all that?"

"Okay, *stop*," I hiss as loudly as I dare, before Drew can snap back at Alonso. There's one way I can end their argument, but it involves offering up way too much personal information. So I decide to go with the other option: grumpiness. "I *don't care* if this stupid Resistance exists. My arms are getting tired, and we have to decide if we're sneaking out of this tunnel right now or not."

"We could wait until nightfall," Louisa suggests. "So we'd be less likely to be spotted?" I could tell she was mystified and bored by the Resistance conversation. Following politics is not Louisa's strong suit. Yet another thing I like about her. She wouldn't understand some of the details of my life story, but she'd be my friend regardless. And she'd understand the really important things, like about Wren. Not that I can tell her any of it, of course.

"That's a good idea," Ryan says. He gives Louisa a

big smile, but she doesn't notice because she's crouching to check on Maddie again.

"No, sorry — I mean, it is a good idea, Louisa," I say, "but we can't wait that long. The Alliance might use the tunnel before then." I peek back out at the boxes. Nobody is near them, but I can't imagine why else they'd just be sitting there. I'm afraid that any minute a crew of soldiers will show up and start carrying them into the tunnel.

"Can you see anywhere for us to hide?" Drew asks me.

I scan the area again, watching the soldiers for longer this time. Most of the activity seems focused around two distant buildings: a big one, which I'm guessing is the mess hall, because people keep coming in and out with plates of food or tin mugs, and a smaller one, which over-looks a field on the far side of the camp. Soldiers are jogging around the field or doing push-ups and jumping jacks in the middle of it.

"I think we've arrived during breakfast," I say. "And morning calisthenics for the other half of camp. There are a couple of small buildings and tents near us that might be empty." I lower the trapdoor again and shake my arm out, thinking.

They're all looking up at me, six worried faces. I don't love what I'm about to suggest, but I don't think I have much choice. If I want them all to follow me, I have to lead. I always figure that's better than following someone else.

"Here's what we'll do," I say. "I'll make a run for the nearest building by myself and peek in the windows. If the coast is clear, I'll signal for you guys to follow me. Okay?"

"What if it's not clear?" Louisa asks.

"I'll find another building where it is," I say, trying to sound confident. "Just watch for me."

"What if you get caught?" Maddie asks, twisting a lock of brown hair around her finger.

Now, there's something I really don't want to think about. "Then come get me," I say with a smile. Then I glance outside again, make sure no one is watching the trapdoor, and shove it open just far enough to wriggle out.

Drew climbs up the rungs right below me, his arm behind my shoulders, holding the trapdoor ajar as I squeeze through the gap. I wish it were anyone but him keeping an eye on me, but there's not much I can do about it. At least he's strong. I crawl free and he lowers the trapdoor quietly behind me.

Immediately I roll into a crouch and run to the boxes, which provide the nearest place to take cover. On one side they face a tall wire fence, not far from a large double gate, with woods pressing up against it that look exactly like the ones we were just walking through last night. I crouch on that side for a moment, peeking out at the rest of the camp.

That's when I see the guards off to my left. More important, I see the building they're guarding, and I see the bars on its windows, and I see the thin figures in black walking in slow circles in a small yard behind another barbed wire fence.

That's a prison.

The Alliance is keeping some of its prisoners in this camp.

Which means . . . which means that at this exact moment, I could be heartbeats away from my sister, Wren.

Chapter 7

Every atom in my body wants to leap out from behind those boxes and run right over to the prison. I want to grab one of those rifles from the guards, bash down the doors, and scream Wren's name over and over until she comes running out and I can throw my arms around her and she can be the one in charge again. How many times have I promised the universe that I would never fight with her ever again if I could just have her back? How many gifts have I offered to give up in exchange for seeing her once more?

I wouldn't care if we got caught; I wouldn't care who

had us or what they did with us, as long as we could be together.

But it's not just me here. I wouldn't call most of them friends, but there are still six other people underground right now who just want to get to safety. They're counting on me not to, you know, freak out and attack some prison guards.

I wonder if they would mind waiting there while I ran over and spied on the prison. I so desperately want a closer look at the people on the other side of that fence. If I could talk to one of them, even, maybe someone inside would have seen a nineteen-year-old girl who looks like me but prettier, with a smile that would have made her a movie star back when they still made movies.

But I can't leave Louisa and the others in the tunnel. Someone could come along and open that trapdoor any minute. We need to find a safer hiding place, and then we need to find a way out of here.

Perhaps if I can stash the others somewhere, then I can go check out the prison.

Or if we find a way out, maybe I can let them go on without me, while I stay and look for Wren.

I force myself to scan the nearest buildings. There's a small guard shack next to the gate, about ten long strides away from me to my left, but through the tall open window I can see that it's empty at the moment.

Beyond that, between the gate and the prison, there's a large camouflage canvas tent, which is probably a dormitory. It faces the prison, away from the boxes and the gate, so the occasional soldier going in and out of it won't see me as long as I stay in the shadows and don't move.

Along the side of the tent, close to the fence, is a scraggly pen with several black-and-white goats, a bunch of scrawny chickens, and one tall, grumpy-looking bird with giant feathers. It takes me a minute to recognize it from the pictures I've seen in books: an ostrich. The Alliance must have taken it from one of the last remaining Canadian zoos. Ostrich eggs are probably huge; I bet one egg could feed ten soldiers.

Okay, I'm totally making that up, but why else would they have an ostrich?

Ahead and to the right of me, between the boxes and the big central field of the camp, are a few low buildings, most of which have steps and doors on the sides. The closest one is only a short dash across a sunny stretch of grass, so I take a deep breath and run, throwing myself down into the shadows below it and slamming my eyes shut, hoping nobody saw me.

There are no shouts of alarm, no rifles poking me in the gut, so after a minute I let myself breathe and open my eyes again. Back at the trapdoor, I can just see Drew's eyes peeking out at me. I think he looks amused, although I really can't tell from this distance, so it's possible I'm just looking for reasons to get mad at him. Then again, he's the type to find my heroism amusing, so I frown at him, anyway.

The window on the back wall of this building is a

little too high for me to see into, so I have to roll a large rock over and stand on it on tiptoes. I grab the windowsill with my fingertips and poke my nose over the edge.

It's only one room, and it must be some kind of filing storage space, because there are piles of papers all over the two desks and the wooden floor. What is with the Alliance and paper? Why can't they use digital storage like normal people? I guess this way they don't have to worry about accessing everything when they don't have electricity. And piles of papers can't be hacked. Or wiped out by electromagnetic pulse attacks, like the ones that wrecked all the electronic equipment in Seattle, Cardiff, and Mumbai a few years ago.

Still, come on, Alliance, join the twenty-first century already. Making kids learn to write with pens and pencils again is just cruel. I swear my right arm is still sore from two weeks of relearning to use a pen at CMS.

A movement in the room makes my heart leap up and bang into my throat. Before I lose my grip from the fright, I see that it's a guy, probably in his early twenties, sorting through some papers with a fierce expression. Then my fingers slip and I tumble back, staggering off the stone and landing on my knees on the dirt beside it. I hold my breath for another minute, waiting to see if anyone heard the thud or saw my graceful crash. But apart from Drew's eyes at the trapdoor, no one seems to be looking my way.

I stick out my tongue at Drew and then slide my hand across my throat, shaking my head. *Not this building. Not safe.* I wave for him to stay put, peek around the side of the building, and sprint to the next one over.

Here we're a bit luckier. There's a drainpipe I can stand on to hoist myself up to the window, and immediately I see that there's no one inside. I'm guessing this is where the boxes were stored until they were moved outside. The room is mostly empty, but the floor is free of dust, as if there were something on it not too long ago. A few stray cans and smaller boxes are scattered across the shelves that line the walls. The only sign of life I see is a gray mouse sauntering boldly around, scavenging for crumbs.

There's nothing in the room that the soldiers will come looking for. It looks like a perfect place to hide, at least until we figure out what to do next.

I beckon to Drew, then slip around the side, up the steps, and in through the door as quickly as I can. The mouse sits up and stares at me, as if it's rather offended I've come to disturb its stolen meal. It looks even more displeased when Ryan thumps through the door behind me, followed by Evelyn, Alonso, Louisa and Maddie together, and finally Drew with my backpack. If I'd been back in the tunnel, I would have made them wait longer between people, but we swing the door shut and wait and there's no reaction from outside. So I guess we're safe for the moment.

"This is perfect," Louisa says, exhaling. She sets down her backpack and pats the faded red wall. Flakes of paint drift to the floor. "See, Maddie? We're going to be okay."

She sounds like she's reassuring herself as much as anyone else.

Maddie rubs her arms and looks around the small, dark space as if she's not convinced.

"What else did you see out there, Rosie?" Evelyn demands, her dark eyes shining with excitement. She peeks out the back window, but there's not much to see in that direction besides the gate and the pile of boxes. There's a dirty front window out onto the rest of the camp, but none of us want to get too close to that in case we're spotted.

I tell them about the guard shack, the tent dormitory, the prison, and the filing storage in the building next door. Evelyn and Alonso both light up at this last bit of information.

"There could be important documents in there!" Alonso says.

"We should steal some!" Evelyn says, and he nods. "To take back to the Resistance!"

"And how do you plan to get these hypothetical papers to this imaginary band of merry rogue heroes?" Drew says snidely.

"I don't know. Maybe we'll post them on the Internet," Evelyn responds in the same spiteful tone.

"Well, it's not safe to go in, anyway," I point out, trying to stop them from arguing again. "There's a guy in there right now."

"I'll watch for him to leave," Alonso immediately volunteers. He hurries over to the door and holds it slightly ajar so he can watch the building across from us.

"All right, well, while you do that very important thing," Drew says, "the rest of us can figure out how to get out of here. Any ideas? Rosie, do you think that fence goes all the way around the camp?"

"I'm pretty sure it does," I say. "Especially since they have prisoners to keep in, besides protecting the soldiers from outside attack."

This makes the others look, if possible, even gloomier.

"Maybe we should wait until dark and go back into the tunnel," Ryan suggests. "If they can use it to get across the border, we can, too. And what are the chances they'll use it at night?"

"Why wouldn't they?" Louisa says. "I don't know. . . . I don't want to go back down there if we can help it. I felt like a rat trapped in a maze. And we'd have nowhere to hide if Alliance agents came from either direction."

"We can't stay here," Maddie says. "They'll catch us any minute."

We're clearly about to have a serious morale problem. What everyone needs is some strong leadership. Even if I don't have any brilliant ideas, I can at least give them that.

"All right," I say, "Louisa, you and Maddie take turns keeping an eye on those boxes out the back window. I bet they'll be going into that tunnel soon, so watch for who takes them and when, and maybe then we can figure out how often they use the tunnel." I turn to Evelyn. She's going to be obsessed with her dopey document-stealing plan, anyway, so I know it's pointless to give her anything else to do. "You and Alonso can keep watching the file storage place next door. But don't do anything risky or stupid. Remember that getting us out of here is more important than stealing anything, no matter how useful you think it might be."

"But we could stop the War!" Evelyn protests. "We could be heroes!"

"Not if we're thrown in an Alliance prison — like, for example, the one right here," I point out. "So let's focus on that first. Ryan, you watch out the front window to make sure no one is coming this way. And Drew, you check these last few boxes to see if there's anything edible in there. I'll go scout around the camp and see what I can find out."

"Um, I don't think we should eat anything in here," Drew says. He points to the floor, and I follow his gaze to the little gray mouse.

"Ew!" Louisa cries.

"The poor thing!" Maddie gasps.

The mouse is lying flat on the floor in the center of the room, and for a horrifying moment I'm sure it's dead. I immediately wonder where a giant stash of poisoned food could possibly be going.

Then I see the mouse's small furry chest rise up and down, and I realize it's sleeping. Drew pokes it gently with the toe of his boot. "Still alive," he says. "But at least some of the food that was in here must be drugged. I don't want to risk it, do you?"

We all shake our heads. I'm even more mystified than before. What is the Alliance planning? Who are they going to put to sleep with that food? I'd sort of figured the boxes might be going to CMS, since the schools are the closest places to the other side of the tunnel. But why knock out a bunch of teenagers? The four of us managed to get out just in time, but I doubt anyone else will even try to escape, especially since the teachers will be on high alert because of us.

I glance at the logo on the boxes again. Does the US government know that NutriCorp is involved with the

Alliance? I've seen their stuff in grocery stores everywhere. They could start drugging the whole American population without anyone realizing it.

"So I'll come with you," Drew says, jerking me out of my thoughts.

"No!" I say, too fast, and they all look at me as if I've just bitten Drew's ear off. "I mean — I just mean, I'll be safer on my own. Harder to spot." That is true. It's also true that I don't trust Drew at all. Not only that, but what I really want to do is get close to that prison. I don't want to explain why to anyone else.

But Louisa and Ryan are both shaking their heads. "You'll be safer together," Louisa says. "Please, Rosie. I'll be so nervous if you're out there alone. What if you don't come back? Then what do we do?"

"Drew can watch your back," Ryan says. "He's a great tracker. And he might see something you don't."

Okay, now I'm offended. Remember how I didn't want any boys on this escape with us? Here's one reason why. They always think they can do things better than girls can, and guess what? They're wrong. I guarantee I can shoot straighter, start a fire better, and climb a tree faster than Drew or Ryan or Alonso. And Wren was better than Ivan at everything — except lying, I suppose.

I want to argue with them, but I know it's no good. Drew is going to follow me whether I want him to or not.

"Then you'd better keep up," I say to him, and I'm out the door before he can give me one of his smug expressions.

He catches up to me as I duck inside the guard shack. I was hoping to find something that would open the big gate, but there's no magical ring of keys hanging helpfully from a hook on the wall. There aren't any bolt cutters for the huge links of chain that hold the gate shut. There's no giant button that says: PRESS ME TO ESCAPE! It's just a tiny room with a broken swivel chair in it.

I'm guessing they don't use this gate very much. I wonder if we could climb over it without getting spotted, but we'd have to deal with some wicked coils of barbed wire at the top, which would be the very opposite of fun.

I glance out the window as Drew crowds into the room with me. From this angle I can see clotheslines tied to the back of the dormitory tent, stretching between the tent poles and the fence posts of the animal enclosure. Several Alliance uniforms are hanging up to dry, most of them still pretty wet. I always thought the Alliance had plenty of access to electricity, since they control most of the fuel companies, but I guess even they save electricity by making their soldiers do laundry by hand. My family does that, too, but we pay someone else to do the hard work.

Drew figures out what I'm thinking without me having to say anything. "Let me get them," he whispers. He darts out and runs to the clotheslines, where the flapping shirts and trousers hide him from sight for a moment. At least, from me and the rest of the camp, but I see the ostrich and a couple of the goats whip around and stare beadily at the laundry. Drew's lucky they can't get out, because they look like they're itching to pick a fight with an intruder.

I turn my gaze to the prison. Now would be a good time to try to shake Drew and take off on my own, but I'll be able to get closer if I'm disguised as a fellow soldier. So I wait until he comes scurrying back with two jackets, two pairs of pants, and a hat. We struggle into them, and of course they're too big, although he clearly chose the smallest ones he could find. On the plus side, that means I can put them on right over what I'm wearing. He tosses me the hat.

"In case they make the girl soldiers cut their hair," he explains, pointing to my long dark hair. I twist up my hair and tuck it under the hat. Fine, that was smart thinking. But I'd have come up with it myself; I don't need him.

"Let's split up," I suggest. "I'll go that way." I nod toward the prison. "You see what's going on in the other direction."

He gives me a weird look. "The only thing that way is the prison. Let's follow the fence and see if we can find a front gate to this place."

"Okay, great idea. You do that," I say. "I'll catch up to you in a minute." My gut says to stay with him and keep an eye on him, but I can't fight how much I want to check that prison. I know it's crazy. There's a part of me that knows, logically, that there must be plenty of Alliance prison camps. What are the chances Wren will be in this one, where I happen to show up? But if I can find out anything about her . . . Knowing *something*, anything at all, would be better than the last three awful years of knowing nothing.

Drew studies me, and now he looks like Ivan again, but in the way Ivan's know-it-all look could suddenly turn understanding. Ivan looked at Wren that way whenever she told him about her dreams of saving the planet — the protests she wanted to organize, the petitions and poems and videos, the evidence she wanted to take to the people in charge so they'd actually do something about all the homes that have been destroyed by the superhurricanes and earthquakes and rising oceans.

When Ivan looked like that, it was impossible to imagine he wasn't on our side.

But I know better now. I'm not going to fall for a sympathetic expression again.

"What is it?" Drew asks. "What do you think you're going to find over there?"

"No one," I blurt, and his eyebrows shoot up. "I mean, nothing. Look, just do as I say. We don't have time for arguing."

I pull the hat down so the brim shades my eyes and I march out of the guard hut before he can say anything else. I try to walk past the front of the dormitory tent like I belong here. There are enough uniforms wandering around that I should be able to get by if nobody stares at me too closely.

There's a cold wind whipping through the tents, even though the sun is bright overhead. I'm glad for the thick khaki jacket over my hoodie, and the heavy khaki pants over my still-damp jeans. My sneakers are finally starting to dry, but they're still uncomfortably chilly as I stride across the patchy grass.

Two soldiers stand guard outside the prison door, chatting to each other. There are about fifteen prisoners out in the prison yard, most of them stamping their feet or rubbing their arms to stay warm. None of them are talking to one another. I slow down and study each of them hopefully, but disappointment washes over me as I realize they're all men. Either there aren't any women in this prison, or they exercise at a different time.

Still, they might know something. There's only a tall chain-link fence between me and them. If I can stand next to it without the guards noticing, and if I can get the prisoners' attention, hopefully I can talk to one of them, at least for a minute.

I'm walking past the guards, carefully not looking at

them, heading for the fence, when somebody suddenly takes my elbow in a firm grip and marches me straight past the prison. Fear makes my head spin and my muscles tense.

The Alliance has caught me!

Chapter 8

All I can think is, *What will happen to the others? Can they escape without me?* I hope Evelyn doesn't do anything risky. I hope Maddie can keep it together. I hope Louisa doesn't worry about me. I hope the boys don't wreck everything for them.

Then I'm shoved into another small guard hut, next to another tall gate and just as empty as the first one. I spin around and find myself face-to-face with Drew. He looks mad, but I guarantee he's not as mad as I am.

"Are you crazy?" I nearly yell. I'm so furious I could kick him, but I'm also shaking with relief. I pull off the hat and rub my face, trying not to scream.

"Are *you*?" he asks, closing the door behind us. "What were you going to do? Talk to the prisoners? You really think no one would have noticed?"

"Maybe," I shoot back. "You don't know. You didn't have to barge in and ruin it and give me a heart attack." I sit down in the rickety chair, fold my arms, and glare at him. I don't care that I feel like a teenager arguing with her annoying dad. It's an improvement over the feeling I had a few minutes ago, that everything was over for good.

"I was saving your butt," Drew snaps.

"Who asked you to?" I say. "I can handle this. It'll be worth it."

"What will?" he asks. "What's worth taking a risk like that?"

I press my lips together. If I haven't even told Louisa about Wren, why would I tell stupid Drew?

His face changes, the scowl vanishing like his forehead has swallowed it up. "Come on, Rosie. Tell me. Who are you looking for?"

99

Then again, if I don't tell him, we're apparently never going to get anywhere.

I sigh and lean my elbows on my knees. "My sister, okay? And don't you dare tell the others."

"I won't." He crouches beside me. "Why do you think she's here?"

"She has to be somewhere." I glance out the window and see the line of prisoners filing back inside. Oh, great. Now I've missed my opportunity, and it's all Drew's fault. Angry, I turn back to him. "This is the closest we've ever gotten to Alliance prisoners. Do you know how much money my family has spent looking for her? And for nothing! No one knows anything! We don't even know for sure if they have her. And maybe I could have found out — maybe someone could have told me — maybe she's even here —" I run out of words and have to shove my hands against my eyes, forcing myself not to cry.

I'm not going to cry until I see her again. That was what I promised myself three years ago. I'm going to be all thorns and no roses, tough and prickly. Wren used to tease me about that whenever I was mad or sulking. "What did you say your name was?" she'd joke. "Thorny?"

But after the tsunami, after we lost everything, or thought we had, she hugged me and said my thorns would keep me strong until we found a home again.

Then she left, and as far as I'm concerned, there's no such thing as home without her.

"How did they get her?" Drew asks, and I'm glad he doesn't pat my shoulder or tell me it'll all be okay.

"She ran away," I say. "With this guy Ivan, her boyfriend." I leave out the part about our town being destroyed. That would invite too many questions, like *What town was this, exactly?* Wren thought she was running away to make a difference in the world, to stop things like that tidal wave from ruining any more lives. But Drew doesn't need to know that.

I shake my hair back and twist it under the hat again. "She left a note that they were going to join the Resistance. She said Ivan was one of them, that he would take her to them. But we think he gave her up to the Alliance instead."

"Because the Resistance isn't real," Drew says.

"No, they are," I say. "Sorry — you lose that argument. I've met some of them." He doesn't need to know how, or where, or, most important, why. "They'd never heard of Ivan. And they said Wren never found them. We have no idea what happened to her after she left us." I point out the window. "But I have a pretty good guess. And I'm going to find a way into that prison, no matter what you do to try to stop me."

He's already shaking his big fat head. "It's too dangerous," he says. Mr. Cliché. I really can't stand this guy. "I get it, okay, Rosie? I get that you want to find her. But if they catch you, they'll catch all of us."

"Not necessarily," I say.

"Remember what you said to Evelyn?" he says. "Nothing risky. This is way too risky. Stay alive first; do crazy brave things later."

All right, I do kind of like that he calls me brave . . .

even if it comes paired with crazy. But I don't care about his clever points or how many of my words he throws back in my face. He's not going to change my mind. I'm about to point this out, when a strange coughing rumble interrupts us.

We both freeze, listening. It sounds like the bus that took us to CMS, but with more of a deep mechanical rattle. It's definitely some kind of vehicle. I scramble up and lean out the window.

"It's a truck!" I whisper back to Drew. "A *huge* truck!"

A gigantic, wheezing monstrosity, half off-white and half rust, is chugging along a dirt road through the woods on the other side of the fence. As I watch it bump and bounce over the path, I realize it's headed for the gate near the trapdoor.

Then I spot the NutriCorp logo on the side.

"The boxes!" Drew and I yelp at the same time.

"They're not going into the tunnel at all!" I say.

"That truck is taking them away," he says, and I can tell his brain is galloping along right next to mine. It is awesome that I don't have to spend an hour explaining my new plan to him.

"Probably back into the States," I say. "Right across the border."

"Think there's room for seven smugglers in there?" he asks with a grin.

I'm tempted to observe that it would have been much easier to stash four people in there instead of seven, but he looks so pleased that I decide now is not the time for a fight. "We have to get back to the others," I say, standing and reaching for the door.

"What about the prison?"

I stop, one hand on the handle. *Stay alive*, says one side of my brain. *Find Wren*, says the other.

This could be our only chance to escape.

This could be my one chance to find my sister.

The others will never make it to Chicago without me.

But maybe they will. . . . Louisa is a lot more capable than she realizes.

It's the thought of Louisa that makes up my mind. I

guess maybe I like her more than I knew I did. One thing's for sure: I can't abandon her. I can't leave Maddie or Evelyn, either. I know how I felt when I woke up and Wren was gone. I'm not going to do that to my roommates.

I turn and glare at Drew. "Fine. Forget the prison. We escape, now. Do *not* give me one of your smug faces about this." I fling the door open, and we hurry around the back of the prison and the dormitory tent, following the line of the fence together.

The truck is just backing through the fence as we sneak between the hanging laundry on the clotheslines. Two soldiers have pulled the gate open, and two others are standing by the boxes with their sleeves rolled up, ready to load the cargo. I catch a glimpse of a pale face in the window where we left the others — I'm guessing Maddie — before she ducks out of sight.

A stocky woman in a navy blue jumpsuit gets out of the truck with a clipboard and starts talking to one of the soldiers as the other three roll open the back and begin transferring the boxes inside. We don't have long; it's a job that won't take them more than half an hour. But how can we get them away from the truck long enough for us to sneak into it?

"If I had a rifle," I whisper, "maybe I could shoot something and they'd have to go investigate." I glance at the back of the tent beside us, wondering if there are any rifles in there.

"It has to be something that'll get all of them to leave," Drew whispers back. "Do you think they'd all chase me if I ran past them? I mean, if I take off the uniform?"

I shake my head. "Not all four of them. Definitely not the truck driver. And besides, what would happen to you then?"

"My mom's kind of important," Drew says. "Once they figured that out, they'd probably be pretty welcoming."

I wonder who his mom is. I also wonder if he's volunteering like this because he wouldn't mind getting caught, since he's really on the Alliance's side. Is this his chance to turn us in? Did he stop me from going to the prison because there's something going on he doesn't want me to know?

I have to stop thinking in circles like this. Drew hasn't done anything obviously untrustworthy yet. It's just a gut feeling I have, and I know that's mostly because of how he reminds me of Ivan. But it doesn't mean I'm wrong. He could be trying to win our trust for some larger purpose. Maybe he'll call in the Alliance to get us later, once he gets some useful information out of us. I really shouldn't have told him about Wren.

"Hello?" he says, waving his hand in front of my face. "Anyone in there? We have to do something, and quick."

"I know. I'm thinking," I say. "I vote no on making them chase you." I look around, wishing again for a rifle, or better yet, a grenade. We learned about all kinds of homemade explosives at CMS. But there aren't exactly a ton of ingredients within reach.

"BLEEEEAAAAAGG!"

107

Drew and I both jump as a loud, peculiar noise sounds right next to us. I lift aside a flapping bedsheet and find myself staring at a furry nose and sharp black eyes. The goat regards me solemnly from inside her pen. Her face practically says, *Seriously? You didn't think of me right away?*

I glance at Drew, who is grinning — an entirely new expression on him, and one that doesn't look half-bad. Not that I care or notice or whatever.

"Perfect," I whisper.

"You get the gate," he says. "Then go for the others. I'll freak out the animals."

He unclips the bedsheet and heads off to the back of the pen with it. I follow the chicken wire around until I find the spot where the handlers must go in and out. There are a few twisty-ties holding the door shut, and that's it. I glance around, but no one is looking my way. Quickly I untwist the ties and peel back the wire until there's an opening big enough for an ostrich to run through.

A couple of the chickens immediately strut over to see whether I have any food, but the goats and the ostrich ignore me. That part's up to Drew.

I hurry away from the pen and stroll around the front of the buildings so the soldiers by the truck won't notice me. They're all too busy loading boxes to see me slip into the cabin where I left my roommates.

"There you are!" Evelyn explodes as I close the door behind me. "We've been totally freaking out!"

"Well, some of us have," Louisa says, rolling her eyes.

"We've got a plan," I say. "But we have to move fast." I cross to where Maddie is looking out the back window. There's still no movement from the animal pen. Where is Drew?

"Where's Drew?" Ryan asks, echoing my thoughts.

"Working on something. Everyone grab your packs and get ready to run. As soon as the coast is clear, we're getting in that truck." I point out the window.

"Whoa," Alonso says. "I get it. Like fugitives hiding from the law in one of those old movies!" He bumps fists

109

with Ryan, and I think to myself that he can't possibly have a secret like mine, or he wouldn't be able to joke about stuff like that.

That's when I notice that Evelyn is clutching a sheaf of papers to her chest. "Uh-oh. Did you actually —"

"I did!" she says, her dark eyes sparkling. "You should have seen me, Rosie! I was so brave! Like you! Alonso saw the guy leave, so I ran in there, grabbed everything that looked important, and ran back out. Check this out. . . . It's a map, and I think it might show where all the secret training camps are! See, that's CMS —"

I hear a shout from outside and have to interrupt her. "That's totally amazing, Evelyn, but we need to go. You can tell me about it later." It *is* kind of amazing that she managed to do that without getting caught, and if she's right, that would be really valuable information to the Resistance.

Then again, as soon as that guy comes back and finds important papers missing, it's going to set off all kinds of alarms. We could be in a lot more trouble than we were before. But it won't do any good to tell her that. Better to make her feel proud of herself. Our team will work better if we can avoid sulking, worrying, or blaming one another.

I check out the window. Seven goats are galloping toward the men with the boxes, bleating furiously. Right behind them is the ostrich, flapping its fluffy wings and squawking. The bedsheet Drew took is tied around one of its feet and whipping around behind it, which seems to be making the giant bird totally crazy. It keeps spinning and stomping on it and nearly falling over and trying to attack its own tail.

The soldiers practically leap out of their skin when they see the animals running toward them. Two of them take off after the ostrich, grabbing for the sheet and ducking away from the bird's angry, stabbing beak. The other two run for the goats, trying to herd them back to the pen. They're shouting for help, but most of the other soldiers in camp are out on the training field or too far away to hear them.

111

The animals scatter with the soldiers in pursuit, and I see Drew sprinting from the animal pen to the truck.

"Time to go!" I say. I do a quick scan out the door, then send Louisa and Maddie out first. Drew reaches the truck at the same time as they do, and he and Louisa throw Maddie inside and then scramble in behind her. The three of them start rearranging boxes at top speed, making a tunnel to the back.

"Okay, Ryan, you next," I say, beckoning to him. He runs to the truck with Drew's backpack slung onto his other shoulder. Alonso gives Evelyn's hand a quick squeeze before he runs after them. She stuffs the papers into her pack and then stands beside me. I wait a moment until it's hard to see the other five behind the rearranged boxes.

"Let's go together," Evelyn says, taking my elbow. I don't know if she's scared, but it gives me kind of a dumb warm, fuzzy feeling that she wants to stick with me.

"You bet," I say. "Since you're an expert at this stealth business now." She grins.

We're out the door and down the steps, nearly half-way to the open truck door, when suddenly I spot the truck driver. I'd forgotten about her completely. She's been standing by the driver's side door, laughing and watching the soldiers chase the goats, but as Evelyn and I sprint across the grass, she turns in our direction.

It's like a slow-motion horror film. There's nothing we can do. In another ten seconds, she'll see us, and the whole plan will be ruined.

Chapter 9

I'm frantically tossing aside options in my head, but before I can do anything, Evelyn barks, "Hey, you, there!"

The truck driver sees us and looks as startled as I am. She squints at Evelyn and me. "Who are you?"

"Who am *I*?" Evelyn says with grand indignation. "*Me?* Did you really just ask me that? Who am *I*?" She gives me an outraged look. "Did you hear that? She doesn't know who *I* am!"

I fumble to play along. "Gosh. Uh, wow. Shocking. Bet your dad won't be happy to hear about that."

"I'll say! He'll be just furious! What's your name?" Evelyn demands.

The driver is so taken aback by Evelyn's attitude that she seems to forget she's being bossed around by a teenager. "Gladys Cato," she answers.

"Write that down," Evelyn says to me, then sails on while I check my pockets, which of course don't have paper or a pen in them. But neither Evelyn nor Gladys notices. "My dad *will* be hearing about this," Evelyn goes on. "Imagine my own driver not having any idea who I am!"

"Oh, no, miss," Gladys says, rubbing her short blond hair anxiously. "There must be some mistake. I'm here for these boxes. Nobody said nothing about no kid."

"Boxes?" Evelyn says, giving them an airy look as if she's just spotted them. "You mean you're not my ride to Madison?"

"No way," says Gladys. "I'm going to New York. Special delivery. No passengers."

None that you know about, anyway, I think. And also: *Chicago's on the way to New York. Perfect.*

"*Oh*," Evelyn says. "Well, *that* explains that. My goodness. You'd better go tell the guy in there that you're only here for these boxes, then. He was sure you were driving my whole family to Madison. He'll need to see your papers and everything." She points at the filing storage building.

"But I showed them to the other soldier —" Gladys starts.

"Doesn't matter. That's the hierarchy, you know? I mean, *I* should know, with my dad at the top!" Evelyn says. "You'd better hurry, before that guy leaves for lunch."

"Yes, right, okay," says the truck driver. She grabs her clipboard and trots off, looking flustered.

We wait until she disappears into the low wooden building, and then Evelyn and I leap into the truck and scramble through the tunnel of boxes the others have built. They've made a hole near the back wall, with just enough room for the seven of us to sit huddled together. As soon as Evelyn and I are clear, Ryan and

Louisa shove boxes around to fill in the tunnel, until it looks from the outside like a solid wall of boxes.

"That was awesome!" I whisper to Evelyn. "How did you do that?"

"I always thought I should be an actress," she says, beaming. "You know, there used to be a famous improv group in Chicago. My mom told me about it. I think I would have been perfect for it, don't you?"

"Yeah, totally," I say, and I really mean it. For the first time, Evelyn's actually impressed me.

"Maybe if the War ever ends," she says ruefully.

"But what if the guy in the building says he doesn't know anything about a family going to Madison?" Alonso asks. "Won't they get suspicious?"

"There's no one in there," Evelyn says. "Hopefully Gladys will decide she needs to leave before he comes back." She crosses her fingers.

"And now we know something useful," I say. "This truck is going to New York. We just have to make sure we get out when we're anywhere near Chicago."

"How are we going to figure that out?" Maddie asks.

I shrug. "We'll worry about it when we have to." I'm squeezed between Louisa and Drew, with Alonso across from me, so close our toes are all touching. Sunlight from the open back door filters in through the gaps in the stacks around us. Boxes tower over us, but Ryan has stacked them so they're braced and won't fall on us. I hope he knows what he's doing, because getting crushed by a bunch of canned goods is not on my to-do list for this lifetime.

On Louisa's other side, Maddie fiddles with her messy hair bun and yawns. It's warm and getting warmer in the truck, so I wriggle out of the army jacket and tuck it underneath me as a cushion against the hard floor. Now all we can do is wait, and that's just about my least favorite activity.

"I wish we'd had time to find a phone," Louisa says. She clasps her hands around her knees. "I want to call my parents and let them know I'm all right."

Ryan laughs and we all give him a startled look. "Sorry," he says. "I'm just picturing that conversation. 'Hey, Mom, I'm calling to say I'm okay! No, I'm not at school anymore. Well, actually I'm in an Alliance prison camp in Canada. But, you know, hiding in a truck, so everything's great!' I bet your parents would appreciate that."

Louisa and Maddie giggle, and I find myself grinning, too. All right, maybe not all the guys' jokes are stupid and unfunny.

"Shhh," Drew whispers. "I think I hear them coming back."

We all sit there, trying to stay as still and quiet as we can. My right foot starts to fall asleep, and my arms ache from the way I'm leaning on them, but I'm afraid to move in case something scrapes against the metal floor of the truck, or a box shifts and gives us away. The others are frozen the same way. I'm not even sure Maddie is breathing. She looks pale and terrified. Evelyn has her pack half-open and she's holding it like that, motionless, clutching the canvas in tight fists. Alonso and Drew both have their eyes closed, as if that'll help them listen.

We hear the soldiers banging around the outside of the truck, bantering about the goats and the ostrich. One of them jokes that the ostrich bite on his arm should count as a war wound. Another one teases his friend about how girls are even better at running away from him than those goats were. They're all in a good mood despite the animal escape, which would be cute if they weren't the enemy. Unfortunately, I guess they're so cheerful because the War is going their way, and that's really depressing.

The truck groans and creaks as they toss in the rest of the boxes and stack them all the way to the roof. We're pretty stuck in here now. Of course, that's when I notice how hungry I am.

Nobody moves or says anything until we hear the back door of the truck roll down and slam shut, leaving us in the dark. There's a long pause. Slowly I ease my legs into a more comfortable position and rub my prickling foot. Through the walls we can hear the muffled voices of the soldiers and the truck driver. But we can't hear what they're saying. After a while, the driver's door slams, and we feel the vibration of the engine starting up.

"I think it's safe to talk now," Ryan murmurs. "She won't hear us over that." It is a pretty loud engine, coughing and sputtering and roaring. With a jerk, the truck lunges forward, and we all brace ourselves as best we can on the piles of boxes around us. It's going to be a bumpy, uncomfortable ride.

But I still feel a small glow of triumph. We're on our way. Maybe this escape is finally taking a turn for the better. Maybe we'll even make it to Chicago . . . although at this point I'd settle for getting back into the States!

Evelyn fishes a flashlight out of her pack and sets it in the center of the circle, pointing up. The light reflects off the boxes, casting a reddish glow over all of us. We all look kind of weird in the shadows, as if we're telling ghost stories around a campfire — something I've read about, but nobody I know has actually done.

"I'm *starving*," Louisa says. "I didn't realize it before, but it's been ages since we ate anything."

I nod. The adrenaline of our near misses has kept us going, but now that we have a moment to stop and rest, hunger is roaring in my stomach, too.

"Kind of ironic," Evelyn says ruefully. "We're surrounded by boxes of food, but we don't dare eat any of it in case it puts us to sleep."

"Or worse," Alonso agrees. "Where do you think it's all going?"

"In New York? Good question," Evelyn muses. "I'll have to think of all the possible targets. . . ."

"Does anyone have any food?" Louisa interrupts her. "I mean, while Evelyn's, uh, thinking?"

We all dig into our packs and empty out all the food we have into a pile in the middle of our huddle. The boys are much better stocked than we are, since they were prepared for a week in the woods. I'm glad Louisa manages not to make any snarky remarks about me rejecting their food this time around. They've got packets of granola, dried fruit, soy cheese, boxes of juice, nine rather squashed sandwiches, and several cans made of a weird lightweight metal, which contain vegetables and tofu chili and things like that.

All I have are a few protein bars and a box of cookies I grabbed at the Alliance cabin. Louisa must have done the same thing; she has a bunch of little bags of trail mix, several envelopes of hot cocoa, and a hilariously large jar of applesauce. Evelyn just has the sugar packets from her original escape stash. Maddie has nothing at all.

But it's reassuring. At least we're not going to starve right away. And we all have canteens of water, which everyone but Ryan and Evelyn remembered to refill at the cabin.

Louisa flaps a cocoa envelope between her fingers, shaking her head sadly. "Guess this is no use until we can light a fire."

"Yeah, we're not doing that in here!" Ryan says.

"This isn't going to be superdelicious when it's cold, either," Alonso says, picking up a can of tofu chili.

"And how are we supposed to eat the applesauce? With our fingers?" Maddie wants to know. She tries to lift the jar and pretends it's too heavy. "Jeez, Louisa, is this food or a weapon?" I smother a laugh.

"You'll thank me for it eventually," Louisa says with a smile.

In the end we share the cheese, the juice boxes, and the sandwiches, which have a nutty spread on them that isn't peanut butter. Drew says it's sunflower seed butter, with a blackberry jam the guys on kitchen duty had to make themselves.

"That is so cool," Louisa says. "I never got to make jam on kitchen duty! I just had to get up at four thirty every morning and chop melons for fruit salad."

"At least you didn't have to scrub that fruit salad off the tables later, like some of us," I say. "Right, Maddie?"

"That was the worst," Maddie agrees. Back at CMS, we were both assigned to the cleanup crew together, but she never talked to me while we were working. I could tell she didn't like me, so I didn't bother trying to make friends. I don't waste my energy on people who are that tough to crack, and I had Chui-lian and Rae to talk to instead, which was a lot more fun than painful small talk with Maddie. Usually she just pushed her mop around looking miserable.

From the day we arrived at CMS I got the feeling that Maddie would be a downer — she never looked happy, and all the conversations I overheard between her and Louisa seemed to be about how much she hated the school. That was the main reason I usually avoided her outside our dorm suite, but it wasn't until Louisa admitted the truth about their ID bracelets that I started to guess why Maddie might be like that. Now I wonder if I should have tried a little harder to be nice to her.

As the truck bumps and jolts underneath us, she leans her head on her knees, her half-eaten sandwich in one hand. Her brown eyes gaze into space like she doesn't really see the rest of us.

"How long have you lived with Louisa's family, Maddie?" I ask her.

Maddie sighs, and Louisa answers for her. "Six months," she says, rubbing Maddie's back. "Ever since her mom got called up for duty. Her dad's been gone even longer than that."

"No word from either of them," Maddie says. "I don't even know if they're alive."

"I thought —" Ryan starts to say, and Louisa shakes her head.

"No, we're not sisters. We lied about that so Maddie could come to CMS with me. I'm sure your mom is fine, Maddie. And you've got me, right? And my parents love you." Louisa's fingers trace her own neck, and I know she's thinking of the locket she lost the night we escaped. It has her parents' photos inside, and I think it was her grandmother's. Most likely she'll never see it again.

Maddie gives her a sad smile. It occurs to me that Maddie and I have more in common than she knows. We're both missing family members, with no idea what's happened to them, thanks to this war. Maybe one day I'll tell her that, but not now; I don't want to turn the truck into some kind of touchy-feely healing-sharing-weeping circle.

Ryan hefts the jar of applesauce. "Hmmm. Think we could use this to play Spin the Bottle?"

We all crack up, even Maddie and serious-faced Drew. I'm sure none of us have ever played anything like that, and I can't imagine a weirder place to try.

Instead we spend the next couple of hours playing goofy alphabet games, like the one where I say, "Chicago," and then Drew has to come up with a city that begins with *O*, like "Ottawa," and then the next person in the circle (Evelyn) goes, "Albuquerque," and then Alonso says, "England!" and Louisa goes, "BUZZ! Cheat! That's not a city! Disqualified!" and Maddie goes, "Wait, I'm confused. Explain the rules again?" And it's all surprisingly funny, considering our surroundings.

I catch myself thinking that I wish my last border crossing had been this much fun. Which immediately makes me start to worry that I'm not being vigilant enough — that having fun means that something is about to go terribly wrong.

But it's hard not to smile when Louisa smiles, or laugh at Evelyn's impressions of Mrs. Brewster, or joke with the guys about how terrible they are at camping. And the truck just keeps driving and driving. There's a long stop once, which might be the checkpoint where the truck enters the States, but there's no real way to know. We keep very still while we're stopped, but nobody comes back to check on the boxes, and it seems like there's no way anyone could know we're in here.

So finally I let myself relax a little.

After a while I pull out *Julie of the Wolves* from my pack, but reading in moving cars makes me motion-sick, so Louisa and Evelyn take turns reading it out loud to the rest of us. I really like the book, but we didn't get much sleep the night before, so eventually I rest my head on Louisa's shoulder, and one by one we each fall asleep.

Chapter 10

I guess it's the quiet that wakes me.

I open my eyes slowly, confused about why my legs and back are aching and my clothes feel uncomfortably heavy. The flashlight battery has died, so it takes me a moment to figure out why I'm in the dark with people squashed all around me. It's especially confusing because there's no rumbling or jolting underneath us. The truck has stopped, and everything is quiet outside. I fumble around until I find my own flashlight and click it on.

The others are all asleep. Louisa and Maddie are curled into each other; Ryan and Maddie are both snoring gently. Alonso is definitely going to wake up with a sore neck from the way he's positioned. Evelyn has her head on her pack, which is in her lap, as if she's asleep at her desk in school.

Somehow in my sleep I've shifted around, so my feet are tangled up with Maddie's and I'm leaning against Drew. I shake feeling back into my fingertips and carefully wriggle without jostling the others until I'm sitting upright.

Then I realize that Drew isn't asleep. He smiles and shades his eyes when I swing the flashlight toward him.

"How long have you been awake?" I whisper, turning the light down to the floor.

"Since the truck stopped," he whispers back. "I think that was a couple of hours ago."

"Oh," I say. "Sorry I fell asleep on you."

"That's okay," he says. "It's kind of fascinating to see you look so peaceful. Not your normal expression." He grins and stretches his arms, and I realize he's probably been keeping still so he wouldn't wake me.

"Well, don't get used to it," I say, but I try not to sound unfriendly. "I wish I had my watch. What time do you think it is?" My watch was confiscated on the first day at CMS, along with everyone's electronic devices. I spent the first week checking my wrist fifty times a day. It was really annoying.

"I bet it's nighttime," he says, "although I'm just guessing by how hungry I am."

"Oh, yeah," I say, and my stomach growls in agreement.

"She's probably stopped somewhere to sleep."

"So maybe if she doesn't come back soon, we could try sneaking out to see where we are," I suggest.

"That's what I was thinking. Maybe find some more food, too."

"Definitely." There're about a million things I would like to do if we could get out of this truck. Stretch my legs. Change my clothes. Brush my teeth. Run and jump and yell and breathe deeply. And find a phone to call my parents.

If they've gotten a ransom demand from CMS, they must be totally freaking out. It's possible Mrs. Brewster could get something out of them even though I'm not really there, although I hope my parents are smart enough to do that movie thing where they're like, "Prove to me that she's alive! Send me a photo of her with today's newspaper!" Except there aren't newspapers anymore, so maybe it would have to be someone's updated blog instead.

Drew leans over and pokes Ryan's knee. Ryan wakes up with a startled snort. His reddish-blond hair is squashed over to one side from being slept on, kind of like my cat's fur when she first wakes up.

"Let's start moving boxes," Drew whispers to him. "So we can tunnel out."

It's like one of those puzzles where there's an empty space in a bunch of tiles, and you have to slide the tiles around until the picture lines up right. Drew and Ryan and I carefully shift the boxes around us, freezing every time we make a loud noise. We hear nothing at all from outside the truck. I'm hoping Gladys is inside a motel somewhere, snoring away. Worst-case scenario would be she's sleeping in the cab, and then she'll probably catch us any minute . . . but surely she'd rather be in a bed, right?

Anyway, we have to get out, so if she does catch us, we'll just have to run for it.

Soon the movement around them wakes the others, and they get up to help us. Even with all seven of us working, it takes a long time to move all the boxes until there's a tunnel to the back door. By then I'm pretty sure we must be stopped for the night, so I decide it's safe to get out and take a look around.

I have a small heart attack when I first look at the back door and it occurs to me that it might be locked, or bolted, from the outside. What if there's no way out, and we're going to be trapped in here all the way to New York, where they'll open the truck to find us all suffocating, starving, and losing our minds?

But Louisa finds a latch at the bottom of the door almost right away, and when she pulls on it, the door slides right up. It creaks and rattles and rumbles like an

El train roaring over your head in downtown Chicago. I can't believe it doesn't wake everyone in a half-mile radius, especially since the night outside is so quiet.

Moonlight filters down through scattered gray clouds, illuminating a mostly empty parking lot. I jump down to the pavement and stretch my arms and legs like I'm getting ready for a marathon. Everything aches and twinges. I'm not used to sitting all day; normally I make time for soccer or basketball or running or Pilates somewhere in the afternoon. Even on the rare occasions when my parents turned on the TV back home, I liked to stand up and lift weights or jog in place while we watched the news.

As I'm stretching, I scan the area around us. We're in the parking lot of a run-down motel, in a back corner under some trees where the two sputtering fluorescent streetlights overhead don't reach. The truck sits in a pool of shadows by a chain-link fence, across from a long stretch of faded orange doors and windows with curtains tightly drawn across all of them. On the other side of the fence is another empty lot surrounding a warehouse.

I pivot to see the road that runs past the front of the motel. There are a couple of stores and a gas station across the two-lane street, but all the lights are off except for the glow of a lamp inside the gas station's convenience store.

"I think it's safe to come out," I say. "I don't see anyone around. It must be pretty late."

Drew hops down beside me. Louisa and Maddie stop for a moment on the edge of the truck, and I reach up my hands to help them down.

"Ow, ow, ow," Evelyn groans as she hits the ground, hunching her shoulders and twisting her neck to work out the kinks.

"Tell me about it," Alonso agrees.

"We shouldn't all stay out here," Louisa says. "What if Gladys looks out the window? Or a cop comes by and wants to see our ID bracelets?"

"Good point," Ryan says.

"I'll go scout around," Drew offers. "See if I can figure out where we are, or find some more food."

I can't stop myself from thinking he's really going to find a phone so he can turn us in. I know — I feel guilty about it. I mean, he scared an ostrich for us. What more does the guy have to do? But at the same time, there's just something about the way he looks at me, or the way he smiles and ducks his head, or something, that makes me feel jittery and anxious.

"I could go with you," Louisa offers.

"No, I'll go," I say, too fast. I know I'll keep an eye on him better than anyone else can. If he *is* planning something, I'll be the most likely to catch him at it.

Louisa raises her eyebrows at me, then smiles in this girl-conspiracy kind of way. "Sure, okay, Rosie," she says. Her eyes are sparkling, and it takes me a minute to figure out what that face means.

Oh *no*. She thinks I *like* him. Like, *like* him in a boy-friendy way. I want to say, *Man, Louisa, don't you know anything about me yet?* I'm not interested in guys like that.

136

Mostly they just annoy me. I don't have time for hand-holding and guessing games and flirty jokes and waiting around by the phone and moping over how confusing boys are. Plus I've seen how badly it can all turn out, from watching Wren and Ivan. Really, it can't get much worse than having your boyfriend betray you to the Alliance.

I don't know if the guys notice, but Louisa and Maddie are definitely giving each other those silly match-maker smiles I've seen on other girls. Thank goodness it's so dark, so no one can see how much I'm blushing. At least Evelyn seems oblivious — her keen nose for secrets seems uninterested in relationship stuff.

"See if you can find anything else to drink," she says. "And find out what road that is over there. And if we're near any big highways. Here, use this to write down whatever you find." She hands me her small notebook and pencil, then pulls out her map printout and tries to find a patch of moonlight where she can read it.

"Have fun," Maddie says with a grin I just want to mash into her face.

"Yeah, take your time," Louisa agrees. I think she's trying to wink at me. AAARRGH.

"Well, don't take too long," Alonso says. "We should get back into hiding as soon as possible."

"That's true," I say. "You guys stay hidden. Come on, Drew, let's get this over with." I shove Drew ahead of me toward the road and stomp away from the others, trying to ignore Louisa's giggle. I pray to all the spirits of the universe that the others don't gossip about me and Drew while we're gone. That's all I need — five people ooglygooglying over my imaginary romance when they should be focused on hiding and surviving.

We hurry across the lot and head for the main road, staying in the shadow of the motel. Drew keeps looking at my face as if he's trying to figure out whether I'm mad and why.

"Was that weird?" he asks. "Or was it just me?"

"It's really, *really* not important," I say. "Keep an eye

out for signs or even scraps of paper that might give us a clue about where we are."

The big sign in front of the hotel isn't lit up — that would be a waste of electricity — but between the moonlight and the few functioning streetlights we can see that it says CAMELOT MOTEL. VACANCY. A glass door leads into a small lobby at the front. We peek inside, but we don't see anyone at the front desk. Two candles burn quietly on the counter. There are a couple of sad potted plants, a spinning leaflet holder, and a few orange plastic chairs around a coffeemaker and an unplugged vending machine.

"Do you think it's safe to go in?" Drew asks. "What would we say if someone came out to offer us a room?"

I glance around at the deserted street behind us. From the way it's angled, it looks like the view from the desk wouldn't cover the gas station across the road. "We say our parents are across the street getting gas, and they sent us to ask how much a room costs." Not many people drive nowadays, but the ones who do are pretty wealthy, so I'm hoping that'll encourage the clerk to be friendly to us, or, more important, informative.

"Nice," Drew says, nodding approvingly. He doesn't mention how we don't exactly look related, since he's Asian and I'm Hispanic, but I'm betting the motel clerk won't be rude enough to ask. We also have to hope that curfew isn't as strict here as it is in the cities, or else I'll have to come up with a reason why we're traveling so late at night.

It turns out our cover story isn't necessary, though, because nobody appears behind the desk when we walk in. There's a little silver bell on the counter, and we debate ringing it, but I decide it's safer not to talk to people if we can avoid it. I've pulled my sweatshirt sleeves down over my wrists, but I still feel like it's really obvious that I'm not wearing an ID bracelet, which would be just about impossible to explain. Drew keeps his hands in his pockets most of the time, so I bet he's worried about it, too.

A clock on the wall over the coffee machine says it's a little after midnight.

I turn the leaflet holder, flinching at the squeaky noise it makes. I keep my voice quiet. "My mom told me these used to hold brochures about fun places to go, like amusement parks and museums and stuff."

"Amusement parks," Drew says wryly. "I bet those were awesome."

"But a huge waste of fuel," I point out. "Not to mention perfect targets for bombs and stuff like that. It's no wonder they all got shut down when the War started."

"I know, I've heard the propaganda, too," he says. "But I think that stuff's true of most places where lots of people go. My dad says we shouldn't spend our lives being afraid. Like, if we never do anything fun, and if we spend all our time cowering inside our houses, then the Alliance might as well have won already. You know?"

Spoken like someone who's never had to run for his life from angry men with guns. It's easy for guys like him, who don't have to worry that every knock on the door is the end of the world. I'd give up roller coasters any day for the chance to feel safe, just for a few hours. They sound kind of pointless, anyway, from what my mom's told me about them. I've had plenty of real scares and near-death experiences in my life; I don't need to pay for fake ones.

Of course, I don't say any of that to Drew.

I pull out one of the leaflets. Nowadays the government issues these almost every week, and they tell us about new curfews, new restrictions, new things to worry about. This one looks a few weeks old, and it talks about reporting any suspicious activity along the Canadian border and keeping an eye on anyone coming from that direction. It must be from before Canada surrendered, but clearly the government was already worried about Alliance activity over there.

There's nothing on the leaflet to tell us exactly where we are, though. I turn around as Drew leans over the counter to check the desk behind it.

"Mail," he whispers, glancing back at me. He hefts himself up on the counter and grabs a couple of envelopes that were lying in a black plastic in-box. The address on them tells us we're in Wisconsin. I write it down in case Evelyn can find the town on her map.

"Smart thinking," I say, handing the envelopes back to him.

"You would have thought of it in another minute," he says.

I nod. "True." He laughs, but it is. That's the way my brain works, too.

"I like trying to keep up with you," he says. "There aren't many people I'd say that about." In the candlelight his face looks warmer, cuter, all the angles smoothed out and the smugness wiped away. In this moment he doesn't look like Ivan at all, in fact.

"Well, keep trying," I say, patting his shoulder. "You might catch up eventually."

He laughs again, and I feel a weird flutter in my chest. *No, Louisa is NOT right. This is not flirting. This is ordinary conversation with a guy; it's just hard to recognize because I haven't done it in so long.*

I step away from him so he'll stop looking at me like he knows all my secrets. I check the other leaflets, hoping for more recent news about the War, but none of them have been updated recently.

There's nothing else useful in the motel lobby, so we slip out the glass door and run across the street to the gas station. The clouds have slipped down the sky to the horizon, leaving the moon bright above us. It's shockingly cold, but in a clear, bracing way after the claustrophobic stuffiness of the truck.

I check up and down the road as we cross — no cars anywhere, which isn't surprising — and spot an on-ramp to a bigger highway not far away. The sign points to Route 94 East. I stop by the gas pumps and write that down for Evelyn, too.

It takes me only a minute, but when I look up, Drew has vanished.

Chapter 11

I'm not going to panic. I'm not going to panic.

I *am* going to kill him.

So much for my hypervigilance. Was he just waiting for me to get distracted? Where did he sneak off to so fast? And what is he doing while I'm not watching him?

I hurry to the door of the convenience store, but it's locked. So he's not in there, unless he figured out how to lock the door behind him really quickly. I peer in through the glass, but there's no movement in the dark aisles.

"Drew!" I hiss, whirling around. "Drew! Where are you?" The gas pumps are like tall, silent robots, watching me blankly. The little numbers over the nozzles say that gas is sixty dollars a gallon here.

Silence stretches around me. It's so cold even the insects are holed up somewhere. There's a faraway hum like a generator off in the distance. Then I hear a soft *clink* around the back of the gas station.

I pelt around the corner of the store and run right into Drew. He's standing at a pay phone, holding the receiver in one hand as he slides coins into the slot with the other.

A pay phone!

"Hey," he says, giving me the most harmless, innocent grin I've ever seen. "Look what I found! We really are out in the country, huh? It's like a relic from the last century. Who still uses these? Right? But I'm getting a dial tone, so I figured I'd try it."

I glare at him.

"Who are you calling?" I ask. I know I sound accusatory, but too bad; I *am* accusing him. How dare he sneak off like that! He can't have had time to call

146

Alliance agents in the minute I took my eyes off him . . . can he?

"My parents, of course," he says. He looks puzzled, like my anger has confused him all over again. "But no one's answering. They might be traveling for work — they do that a lot. I can't remember their cell phone numbers, though." He hangs up, shaking his head, and coins shower into the slot at the bottom of the phone.

I eye him suspiciously. He can't remember his parents' phone numbers? Or is he lying to explain why he's not talking to someone right now? Did he just hang up on the Alliance? "Seriously?"

"Well, I always use my cell phone to call them," he says. "Their numbers are in there, so I never bothered to memorize them. You know?"

I guess I do understand that. We are crazy about keeping track of one another in my family, so I know all my parents' numbers, but I need my phone to call any of my friends or find their e-mail addresses. Yet another annoying thing about Mrs. Brewster taking away our electronics.

"All right, let me try," I say. But as I pat my pockets I realize I don't have any change. Why would I? It's been ages since I used cash at all — not since we left home, probably. We just use our ID bracelets to charge everything.

It's actually kind of weird that Drew has change. I'll add that to my list of Suspicious Things About Drew, although I can't come up with an explanation that points to Alliance spy.

"Here, use these," he says, passing me his handful of quarters. I slip them in and dial home. My anger at Drew starts to fade as the phone rings and my hopes rise. I could be moments away from talking to my parents! Just the thought makes my throat feel tight, like I'm about to cry, although of course I won't let myself do that.

Ring. Ring. Ring.

Where are they?

Ring. One more ring and I'll get the voice mail.

Should I leave a message? Or save the quarters and try a different number?

Part of me would love to hang on just to hear Dad's voice on the message, but I know I shouldn't. I'm about to hang up when Drew reaches over my shoulder and hangs up for me. The coins clatter down again, and I frown at him.

"Saving the change," he explains.

"I *know*," I say. "I was about to do that. I'm not an idiot."

"Of course you're not! I know!" He raises his hands in a gesture of surrender. "Sorry. Just trying to help."

There's a pause as I scrape the coins out and look at them, heavy in the palm of my hand. Dread is starting to gather like smoke in my stomach, coiling and twisting around my insides. "Why aren't they there?" I say. "It's the middle of the night. Where else would they be?" I hesitate. "Maybe I should try again."

"Sure," Drew says gently, but I stand there for another minute, thinking. What if something terrible has happened? What if they've been found out, and they had to run? They wouldn't have left home — or, worse, the country — without me, surely. But how would they have gotten me a message, out at CMS with no phones or mail?

What would they do about a ransom demand? Would they call the police? Almost definitely not; they wouldn't want the extra questions, and where I come from, calling the police is a guaranteed way to have a kidnapping end with somebody dead.

Maybe they'd call someone else . . . the guys who made our ID bracelets, for instance. Or the Resistance fighters who helped us get to Chicago. That seems more likely . . . but what could any of those people do?

The horrible part is that we all believed I'd be safer at school. Mom and Dad didn't want to send me away, and I didn't want to go. But it was getting so dangerous in Chicago, and they worried about me all the time. I knew they'd be able to focus on searching for Wren if I were tucked away somewhere safe. We thought that sending me to CMS was the right thing to do. Boy, were we wrong.

The pit in my stomach yawns deeper as I imagine my parents turning over the money. We're rich, sure, but not so wealthy that we can spare as much as Mrs. Brewster probably asked for. What if my parents are meeting Alliance agents on some deserted street corner right now, with a suitcase full of cash and no idea that they won't be getting me in exchange? Will the Alliance let them walk away alive from a meeting like that?

Surely it wouldn't have happened that fast. But now the urgency to get home is prickling all across my skin. I feel sick.

"Try another number," Drew says. He reaches out and lightly runs his hand down my arm. Normally I would shove him away, and I still haven't forgiven him for disappearing, but there's something weirdly comforting about his touch.

151

I dial my mom's cell phone. It rings and rings; no answer. I hang up again, collect the coins, and dial my dad's cell phone.

It goes straight to voice mail. I hang up fast, too fast, without thinking, and the machine swallows Drew's change with a self-satisfied *clunk clunk clunk.*

"Oh no!" I cry. I grab the phone, shake the box, press the lever to return the coins over and over again — but nothing works. The quarters are gone. All I'm getting is a dial tone.

"I'm so sorry," I say to Drew. "I didn't think — the voice mail — I should have just left a message." I hang up the phone and lean my head against the wall, pressing my hands into my eyes. "I can't believe I did that."

"It's okay. Don't beat yourself up," Drew says. He leans on the wall beside me, nudging my shoulder with his. "We'll find more change, another phone. Maybe one of the others has quarters. It's not the end of the world."

I take a deep breath and stand up straight. I'm not a pity-party kind of girl. "You're right. Not the end of the world." I turn around and look at the empty road and the empty lots around us. I've never missed my parents as much as I do right now. I breathe in, out, trying to calm down. I look at him sideways. "Nope, I still feel awful."

"Think of it this way," he says. "Maybe it's better you didn't leave a message. Maybe the Alliance has their phones tapped. You could have led them right to us. Eh? See? Really, you were doing the smart thing. Plus we'll probably be in Chicago by tomorrow. So then you'll see your parents and all this will be over."

He's trying so hard, I can't help but smile. "Nice try. You and Louisa could teach optimism classes."

"I think Ryan would prefer that job," he says. Is he implying that Ryan has a crush on Louisa? I give Drew a quick look, but his face doesn't give anything away. That's the feeling I've been getting, too, but I've also noticed that she keeps looking at Alonso, so I'm not sure Ryan has a chance. Unless Alonso and Evelyn . . . Wow, this is

153

a stupid train of thought. We so don't have time for middle school who-likes-who. The other girls might enjoy that, but it's not me at all.

"Let's get back to the others," I say, shaking my head to clear it. "I don't think we're going to find any food here."

"Not without breaking in," he agrees. "And I don't think we should do anything that people might notice. At least not as long as we want to keep hiding in the truck."

We head back across the road. I keep looking back at the gas station, feeling guilty and confused, but also still a bit suspicious. Why did Drew disappear so fast? Was he trying to ditch me? If I hadn't found him quickly enough, would he have called the Alliance to tell them where we were? What if he's only being nice to me to throw me off the scent?

Or . . . what if I do like him, the way Louisa thinks I do?

Right now, it's hard to decide which would be a bigger problem.

Chapter 12

As we pass the motel lobby, I stop, glancing in through the glass doors.

"What?" Drew asks.

"There is one thing I want to take," I say. "Wait here."

I slip inside and pull one of the chairs over to the table with the coffeemaker on it. I climb up on the chair, then the table, balancing carefully so I don't knock anything over. The clock lifts right off the wall. It's as light as a Frisbee, and I feel a flash of gratitude for whoever decided it was worth spending precious batteries on it.

"Sorry, motel people," I whisper to the lobby. But in

the sunless, muffled space in the back of the truck, we need a way to know what time it is.

Drew nods at the clock when he sees it in my hands. "Yes. Totally useful."

"Hopefully they won't notice it's gone until we're far away," I say.

We sprint across the dark parking lot and climb into the back of the truck. Ryan is waiting by the door to roll it shut behind us. He latches it closed again, and we all crawl back through the tunnel to our hidden space.

While Louisa and the guys arrange the boxes to hide us again, I show Evelyn the address we found. She lights up at the sight of the highway number and slides her map toward me.

"I thought we might be somewhere along there," she says eagerly. "Let's see if we can find the town."

We both study the map in the small yellow beam from my flashlight. The lettering on the towns is so tiny it makes my eyes ache. Maddie leans over to help us, her bun of brown hair looking like a flat, messy bird's nest next to Evelyn's tight, neat rows of braids. I don't even want to think about how my hair must look, after two days without a shower.

"There!" Evelyn yelps excitedly, jabbing the map with her finger. "I found it! So let's see. . . ." She takes out a pencil and measures the distance left to Chicago, comparing it to the scale at the bottom of the printout. "Okay, it looks like we're still about three hundred miles from Chicago."

"So we definitely don't want to get out here," Louisa says. "That's too far. We could get closer if we stay put in the truck."

"But what if she doesn't stop near Chicago?" Alonso asks. "What if she keeps driving all the way to New York tomorrow?"

We all sit in a circle, looking at the map and thinking. Louisa unpacks the food and shares it out so we can eat while we decide what to do.

"We don't have many options around here," I say, peeling the wrapper off a protein bar. "Either we walk the rest

157

of the three hundred miles, or we stay in the truck. I wouldn't risk trying to get a lift from anyone else."

"What if we steal the truck?" Ryan suggests.

Everyone stops eating to stare at him.

"I'm serious," he says. "We take it right now and drive the rest of the way to Chicago. Drew and I took Auto Shop at CMS. I bet we could get it going, even without the keys."

Drew is shaking his head. "Probably, but it's way too dangerous. As soon as she reports us, the Alliance will know exactly where we are, where we're going, and what we're driving to get there. They'll catch us long before we reach Chicago."

"Or the cops will," I say. "There aren't too many cars on the roads these days — I think they might notice one driven by a bunch of teenagers. Then we have to explain why we don't have ID bracelets, why we're out after curfew . . ." *Who I am and where I really come from . . .* I shake my head. "I just want to get back to my parents before I have to deal with reporting any of this. You know?"

"Really? I wouldn't mind finding a cop," Maddie says. "They could help us. They'd get in touch with our parents and get us home. Maybe we should be *trying* to do that."

My stomach lurches nervously. I can't explain to everyone why I don't want to involve the cops. They don't know how much trouble I could be in.

"Let's vote," Drew suggests. "Raise your hand if you want to get out here and find another way to Chicago."

Maddie is the only one who raises her hand. She smiles and shrugs like she doesn't really care that much.

"Okay, raise your hand if you vote for stealing the truck," Ryan says. He raises his hand, and so do Alonso and Evelyn.

"All in favor of staying put?" I ask. It's me, Drew, and Louisa. Stalemate.

"So you decide," Louisa says to Maddie.

Please don't say steal the truck, I pray quietly. *Please don't send us out to get caught by the police.*

159

"Oh, dear," Maddie says, twisting her hair around her index finger. "I don't know! What if we get stuck in here and go right past Chicago? They might catch us when they open the truck to unload the boxes!"

"Gladys will have to stop sometime between here and there," Drew offers. "For lunch or to stretch her legs or anything. It's too far for one straight drive. There's a good chance we'll be able to hop out sometime during the day tomorrow. I'd bet on it."

"But —" Ryan starts.

"Okay," Maddie says. "That makes sense. I vote we stay hidden."

I exhale with relief and punch Ryan's knee. "Good work thinking outside the box, though, Ryan. I'd never have come up with an idea like that." *Mostly because it's idiotic, but I'm trying to reassure, not gloat.* "It's pretty cool that you'd know how to start the truck, anyway."

Ryan looks grumpy, as if he really wanted to test out his car-stealing skills. He takes a dried apricot and chews on it, grumbling under his breath. I wonder if I need to

160

try harder to cheer him up, to keep team morale going, but he's been a pretty cheerful guy so far. I'm guessing he'll be back to normal if we just leave him alone for ten minutes.

"So let's sleep in shifts," I say. "That way we won't miss it when the truck starts moving again. When it does, whoever's awake, keep an eye on the time." I set the clock in the center of our circle. "What do you think, Evelyn — four hours to Chicago?"

"Probably more like five," she says. Five is what I thought, too, but I guessed wrong so she'd get to feel smart correcting me. That ought to help if she's feeling stung over being on the wrong side of the vote. But judging from the way she squishes herself in next to Maddie and splits a cookie with her, I don't think Evelyn's going to hold a grudge.

"Great, okay," I say. "Well, I'm wide-awake. I'll take first shift."

"Me, too," Drew says, and I dearly hope he misses the *Oooooooooo* face Louisa gives me.

161

"And, Louisa, you, too," I say quickly. "That way we can all keep each other awake."

Evelyn, Maddie, Ryan, and Alonso wriggle around trying to get comfortable for a while, but they finally fall asleep. I lean my back against the stack of boxes, combing my hair with my fingers. In whispers, I tell Louisa what happened with the pay phone.

"I didn't even think of that," she whispers back. "I don't know a lot of numbers by heart, either. Like my parents at the hospital . . . I totally haven't memorized their work numbers." She fingers the neck of her shirt where her locket would be. "I wish we could call them now," she says, "but I guess we'll be in Chicago tomorrow. That's soon enough. Wow, can you imagine? We'll be sleeping in our own beds tomorrow night!"

We grin at each other. I have a feeling it might not be that easy, but I want to believe her. For a moment I let myself be Louisa, convinced that things will turn out great.

I let myself forget that there's anything dangerous out there, hunting us.

Chapter 13

A few hours later, we wake Alonso and Evelyn for the next shift. But no matter how I shove the army jacket around underneath me, I can't get comfortable, and I can't fall asleep. My mind keeps going around and around, worrying about all the things that could go wrong, feeling bad about losing the quarters, missing my parents, worrying about Wren, hoping we can get out of the truck safely, and puzzling over Drew. He's asleep beside me, his glasses tucked into the neck of his shirt. He doesn't look like a spy. Why don't I trust him?

It's about seven o'clock in the morning when we hear the cab door of the truck slam. After a moment, the engine starts, and the truck backs up, then rumbles forward, speeding up as we reach the highway. The noise wakes everyone, and we split some of the dried fruit and granola for our meager breakfast. With seven people to feed, the food is going fast. But I can't exactly complain, since it was the guys who provided most of it.

We're all tired and sore from sleeping in uncomfortable positions, so it's a much quieter, more boring ride this morning. Evelyn uses a couple pages of her precious notebook to play Hangman with Maddie and Alonso. Drew and Ryan start an argument in low voices about some book they had to read for English. Louisa rests her head on Maddie's lap and falls asleep again.

I stare at the clock. It moves painfully slowly. I want to be home so badly. I want to walk into my own house, hug my parents, pet my cat, sleep in my own bed. I want to stop worrying about the Alliance catching up to us, or what they've told my parents by now.

Five hours later, the others all go quiet, one by one, as they notice the time ticking past noon. If our calculations are right, we should be near Chicago. But Gladys isn't stopping. Evelyn folds and refolds her map between her short, nail-bitten fingers. I wonder if she's telling herself the same things I am: Well, it's an old truck. It's probably going slower than we calculated. We're probably not *that* close to Chicago yet. We still have time. We'll still be closer than we were last night, even if we're on the other side of the city, if she stops anytime in the next couple of hours.

Then, at half past noon, we feel the truck lurch to the right and gradually slow down.

"Pack up," I whisper, pulling the army jacket back on. "If she's just stopping to stretch her legs and grab some food, we might only have a couple of minutes." Evelyn stuffs her map into her pack; Drew finds room for the clock in his. Ryan gets up and carefully slides a couple of boxes aside as the truck jolts and bounces below us. We all brace ourselves as it clatters to a halt and the engine cuts off.

Louisa takes my hand and squeezes it. She has the

flashlight in her other hand, pointed at the boxes between us and the back door. We wait, barely breathing, until we hear the truck door slam again. Gladys's voice goes past, clipped and muffled with occasional pauses, as if she's talking on a cell phone.

As soon as we can't hear her anymore, we all jump up and start moving boxes. It's faster this time, since we built the tunnel last night and only filled it in with a few boxes. In a couple of minutes we're all crouched at the back door.

"I wish we had a periscope," Evelyn whispers. "Like on a submarine? So we could see outside and know what we're jumping into?"

"Totally," Alonso agrees. "There could be a whole crowd of people out there. Or an Alliance guard."

"It doesn't sound like it," Ryan says. He has his ear pressed against the back door. "I don't hear anything. No cars, no voices, nothing."

"The important thing is not to lose each other," I say. "So don't panic. If anyone sees us, we'll run. But stick together — if we have to run, everyone follow me. All right?"

No one argues with me. I hope they'll really do it. I trust myself to assess the situation and figure out how to escape. But it'll be a lot harder if any of the others take off in the wrong direction. I can't lead them to safety and run around them like a border collie herding sheep at the same time.

"Here goes nothing," Louisa whispers. She reaches down, lifts the latch, and rolls the door open.

Bright sunlight dazzles our eyes. The first thing I notice is the mouthwatering smell of food — soy burgers and tofu dogs and things fried in oil. I hop down while my sight is still adjusting and get ready to run. My sneakers hit pavement and I squint around us.

We're in another parking lot, next to a greasy-looking pizza place with a couple of bicycles locked up out front. It's right off what used to be a busy highway, six lanes divided by a concrete barrier, although now it's probably only used by military and supply trucks, and buses like the one that took us to CMS. There are no cars in sight in either direction. Across the highway I can see a large building with walls of broken glass that used to be a supermarket. Some of the big orange letters in the sign swing loose in the wind.

I scan the area, planning our escape.

Big old stores and abandoned strip malls in each direction. A bridge with a tall fence for pedestrians to get over the highway. Patches of grass growing wild, spreading over the old concrete walkways. An old bus stop, covered in graffiti, with cracked plastic walls.

The pizza place looks like the only functioning business in sight. It must get all the truck drivers who go through here.

The others hit the ground beside me. Ryan pulls the truck door shut as soon as we're all out. He's clanking the latch back into place when the door of the pizza place opens.

Gladys steps outside, holding a paper plate with a limp slice of soy-cheese pizza on it in one hand and a can of soda in the other. No matter how much the country falls apart, you can always find soda wherever you go.

She sees us at the same time as we see her. Her whole face falls open: eyes huge, mouth agape. The pizza and the soda can crash to the ground. Even in her shock, she starts fumbling for something at her waist. A phone? A gun?

I'm not waiting around to find out.

"Run!" I yell.

Chapter 14

I bolt toward the highway. My muscles feel weak and useless after sitting in the truck for so long, but fear makes me fast. I don't look back. I hope the others are behind me.

I fly across the first three lanes and sail over the divider. My backpack slams against my ribs as I run. Chilly air whips across my face and I feel like a runaway train, blasting ahead with no way to stop. I'm far too scared to stop.

Out of the corner of my eye I see a figure running beside me. I throw back my hair and glance over; it's

Drew. I wish it were Louisa or Maddie. I want to be sure that they're safe. Neither of them would be all right on their own, or if they got caught.

I burst ahead of Drew, skid into the supermarket parking lot, and risk a look back. The others are only a few steps behind me — I do a quick count — all six of them. Gladys is standing where we left her, shouting after us. Clutched in her hand is a cell phone. Which is better than a gun, but still bad.

"Come on!" I call to my friends. Evelyn's the slowest, but Maddie looks like she's about to faint or collapse in terror or something. I dart back and grab Maddie's hand, dragging her after me. We pound across the lot and I kick aside the broken glass so we can jump through one of the walls of the abandoned supermarket.

Empty shelves loom up around us in the dark. We hurtle past the wide bins where vegetables used to be, past the cold glass doors that used to lead to ice cream and frozen waffles. There are still a few sale stickers and flags sticking out, relics of a time when there was enough food to throw away tons of it every day.

In the back corner, behind the deli counter, I find a door to a dark kitchen and even darker storage closets. The others follow me through and I slow down for the first time, trying to figure out where each of the doors around us might lead.

"Maybe we should hide," Alonso suggests. "There's enough room for all of us in that old walk-in freezer."

"Worst idea ever," Drew says, and I'm so glad I don't have to say it myself that I want to hug him. "The one thing Gladys knows for sure is that we went in here. The Alliance will check this whole place first."

"So we go out the back," I say, nodding at the employee exit door, "and keep running."

I swing open the door and peek out into the parking lot behind the supermarket. The bulk of the building shields us from view of the pizza place. Gladys won't know which way we've gone.

Still, we stay low as we dash across the sunny pavement. Soon we're running behind one of the strip malls. Nondescript doors and rusty fire escapes flash by. The next large building has a sign on the side that says it used to be a bookstore. For a moment I wonder why they needed all that space for e-readers and flash drives, until I realize it must have sold actual books — old-fashioned ones made of paper, like my copy of *Julie of the Wolves* and the others at CMS.

Then there's a stretch of trees, and I risk a look back across the highway. The pizza place is out of sight. No sign of a truck chasing us down, so that's lucky. But I'm sure Alliance agents are going to come swarming into the area within minutes to find us.

"Back across the highway," I order the others. "Hopefully they'll concentrate their search on this side first." We dash across the wide lanes again, vaulting over the concrete barrier. We pelt through several more parking lots and then hit another patch of trees, where Maddie calls for us to stop. She leans over with her hands on her knees, gasping for air.

"I can't run much farther," she says.

I take out my canteen and pass it around; everyone takes a quick gulp of water. Evelyn collapses beside a tall pine tree, rubbing her legs and grimacing. "We need to figure out where we are," she says. "Are we running in the right direction?"

"Or maybe we shouldn't," Ryan says. "Run in the right direction, I mean. Maybe that's what they'll expect us to do."

"I can't believe she saw us," Louisa pants, holding her hair off her neck. "That was the scariest thing that's ever happened to me."

See what I mean? She has no idea what it's like to really be scared — to think your sister might be dead, to worry that you're going to get caught and lose everything at any moment, to watch your whole life get swept away in an instant. I *wish* Gladys were the scariest thing that had ever happened to me.

Although I'll admit that doesn't make me any less scared right now.

"There are signs along the highway," Drew says. "Let's find one that tells us how far the nearest big city is — and hope it's Chicago."

We find one after another ten minutes of running: a rectangular green sign with sunlight reflecting brightly off its silver back. We duck around to the front of it and discover that Chicago is twenty-eight miles away — and we've been running in the wrong direction.

Maddie sighs heavily.

"It's a good thing," Ryan says encouragingly. "They won't expect us to be going this way."

"Unless they count on us being idiots," Louisa says, looking glum.

"We should get away from the highway, anyway," I say. "Now that we know which way Chicago is, you can use your compass to get us there, right, Evelyn?"

She perks up, nodding as she digs the compass out of her pocket.

"So let's head away from the road and try to circle around." I lead the way down an off-ramp and soon we find ourselves in a suburban-looking neighborhood with lots of trees in between the cute little houses. Louisa visibly relaxes, as if it reminds her of home, but all I can think of is the faces that might be behind any of those sweet lacy curtains, watching us and wondering why seven teenagers are roaming the streets together unsupervised. Who will find us first, the Alliance or the cops? Which would be worse for me and my parents?

We don't see any people out and about — maybe nobody lives here anymore — but I'm still relieved when the houses get more spread out and the trees take over. It's easier in the woods to travel in a wide arc, swinging back around to the far side of the pizza place, aiming for Chicago. Evelyn forgets to grumble about her aching legs as she reads the compass intently.

We've been moving as fast as we can for about forty-five minutes when we hear the distant growling above us.

I stop and look up. Cloudless blue sky, warm sunshine, air as clear as you can find these days when everything's so polluted.

Exactly the worst conditions for hiding from a helicopter.

Chapter 15

"Okay, *now* we have to hide," I say, picking up the pace. "Somewhere indoors. These trees are too scattered to give us enough cover." Especially since there are freaking *seven* of us — though I manage not to say that part out loud.

"Inside someone's house?" Louisa asks. She hurries to keep up with me. "Do you think anyone will help us?"

"Not safe," I say. "There must be somewhere else —"

"There!" Maddie points through the trees. A large concrete structure squats beside the road, several yards away. It's our only option. The thunder of the helicopter blades is getting closer.

We race through the trees and across a small stretch of bare pavement. As we get closer, I realize it's a multi-story parking garage. I dart into the shadows of the entrance and turn around to yank Louisa and Ryan in after me. The others just manage to make it inside before the helicopter bursts into view, churning ferociously in our direction.

They can't have spotted us yet. They're just searching, hoping to catch a glimpse of us from the air. We hurry farther into the garage, past thick concrete columns, over painted yellow lines. Space after space, level upon level. It's hard to believe there used to be so many cars on the road that they had to be stacked and packed into garages like this.

"This garage must be attached to something," Louisa points out. "All these parking spaces must be here so people could go somewhere."

Faded arrows on the wall point us toward broken glass doors and dead elevators. We step gingerly through the doorframes and climb the dingy stairs, following the dim yellow circle of Drew's flashlight.

"Oh," Maddie says in a hushed voice as we step out into an enormous open space, crisscrossed with beams of sunshine. A ceiling full of dusty skylights sparkles far above us. Petrified escalators lead up to a balcony lined with glass storefronts. Triangular planters lined with black and silver tiles, crawling with dead vines, are arranged artistically around the walls. All around us, covered in layers of dust, are closed-up carts and door grates and signs in bold, eye-catching fonts.

For a brief moment, looking up at the faraway ceiling and feeling the hushed stillness around us, I think we're in a church. But then I recognize it from stories I've heard my parents' friends tell.

"It's a mall," Louisa whispers, awestruck. I remember the first night I clicked with her, when we joked around about going to a mall like this.

180

"Oh my gosh, *yay*," I say, grinning at her. "I so totally need a dress for prom!"

She grins wickedly back. "And new *shoes*," she squeals. "I mean, I only have, like, forty pairs. My closet is practically empty!"

"I know!" I say. "I was like, should I wear the purple shoes or the pink shoes with this outfit, and then I was all, if only I had shoes that were purple *and* pink!"

Maddie jumps in, her eyes sparkling. "Oh my gosh, you guys, we totally have to find our dresses before we stop for lunch. After all the fro-yo I'm going to eat at the food court, I'm not gonna want to see myself in the mirror."

"Like, whatever!" I poke her in the ribs. "I bet you can't eat as many burgers as I can!"

"Shyeah, but you'll still be the hottest girl at prom," Maddie says, rolling her eyes. "It's so totes unfair how many guys have asked you."

"OMG, we don't have time for boys!" I say. "We have *shopping* to do!"

181

"Like, totally!" Louisa says, throwing one arm over my shoulders. "And don't forget we need new sunglasses! You know, like, for our tennis game later!"

The three of us burst out laughing. Maddie and I collapse onto one of the giant planters, holding each other up and giggling. Louisa tries to sit down next to us but misses and ends up on the floor, which makes us all laugh harder.

"Okay," Ryan says, "something weird just happened."

"Maybe it's in the air," Drew says, rubbing his chin. "Something that infects girls as soon as they step into a mall."

"Is it contagious?" Alonso asks. He gives us a worried look that sets off our giggles again.

"Not *all* girls," Evelyn says. "You don't see *me* acting like an airhead from a twentieth-century movie." She shakes her head, trying not to smile.

"Come on," I say, taking Maddie's hand. "This is the perfect place to hide. Let's look around."

"We can pretend we're normal teenagers from before the War," Louisa agrees, taking Maddie's other hand.

"Does that mean *we* have to giggle about prom dresses, too?" Ryan asks as we start walking along the row of closed storefronts.

"Oh, please," Louisa teases. "You know you'd look hot in sparkly green taffeta."

"Sure, but I'd look hot in anything," he jokes back.

"Oooo, freaky," Maddie says, pointing at a window display where a couple of mostly naked mannequins are still poised, like actors waiting for the spotlight to turn back on.

She drops my hand to go over and look at them, and a moment later I feel another warm hand take mine. I look up into Drew's brown eyes.

"So what color dress are you thinking?" he asks. "You know, so I can make sure the corsage matches."

"Why, you forward young man," I say. "You haven't even asked me yet. How do you know I'll say yes?"

"Resist this face?" he says, pointing to his winning grin. "Impossible. Can't be done."

He might be right about that, I think. I can't help smiling back at him.

"Can you imagine what it was like?" Louisa says, jumping up on a planter and pirouetting. "All that time for people like us to just hang out? Walking around and shopping on the weekends?"

"Going to the movies," Evelyn says wistfully. "Enormous vats of popcorn!"

"And video games!" Alonso says. He hooks his hands through one of the grates and peers in at an old display of computer games.

"Plus staying in school until you were eighteen," Drew says. "Or even longer if you went to college. No enforced military service. No hiding from the Alliance. No seven thirty curfew, no food rationing, no tanks in the streets."

We all go quiet for a moment, thinking about what Chicago will be like now that the Alliance is closer and stronger than ever. Everyone goes to work for the war

184

effort at fifteen, which is only a little more than a year away for some of us. I wonder where we'll all be in two years. Or in four years, when we should have been getting ready for a prom for real.

Once we get back to Chicago, will I see my friends again? Will we all survive this war?

I shake my head. I should focus on surviving the next couple of days first. Somehow we have to get home without getting caught. We know where CMS is; the Alliance doesn't want us sharing that information. If they've figured out what else we might know — about the cabin, or the prison camp, or the truck full of doped-up food heading for New York — they could get really hard-core about hunting us down.

Suddenly I'm so tired I actually feel myself wobbling. I didn't sleep all night, and it's finally catching up to me. Drew takes my elbow and guides me onto a beige padded bench.

"You should rest," he says. "We'll travel faster and safer once it's dark, anyway."

Evelyn nods. "I'm going to scout around in here," she says. "Maybe I can find a more detailed map, so I can figure out the best route to Chicago."

"I'll come with you," Alonso says.

Before I let myself sleep, Louisa and Maddie and I find a corner and change into new clothes from our backpacks. It's just a little thing, but because we've been stuck in the truck with the guys for two days, we haven't had a chance. It's not the same as showering, but wearing clean black cargo pants and a fresh blue shirt makes me feel worlds better.

"You sleep first, Rosie," Maddie says. She spreads my sleeping bag out on the bench. "We need you wide-awake to lead us home tonight."

I give her a sharp look to see if she's making fun of me, but she seems perfectly serious, as if she doesn't mind me being in charge anymore. I guess a lot of things about her don't bother me so much now, either. She's been more of a trouper than I expected. Especially now that I know more about her life before CMS. And there's something about the way she fluffs my pack into a pillow that reminds me of Wren.

"Hey," I say, touching her shoulder. "Um. I just want you to know — I know what it's like. I mean — not knowing . . . losing someone and not knowing what . . ." I have to stop, since stupid tears are trying to climb up out of my eyes again.

Maddie tilts her head at me. "Really?" she says softly. "Who?"

"My sister," I say. "Her name is Wren. We don't know where she is or what —" I stop again and shake my head furiously. "Anyway. The Alliance probably has her. But we'll find her one day."

Unexpectedly, Maddie reaches out and hugs me. Her shoulder blades are like bony wings under my hands. "I know you will," she whispers in my ear. "And I'll find my mom. The War *has* to end eventually. That's what I tell myself . . . and sometimes it helps."

She pulls back as the others come over. Louisa looks confused but pleased to see Maddie and me getting along so well. Ryan unrolls his sleeping bag on the next bench over.

"Nobody do anything crazy while I'm asleep," I say.

"Yes, boss," Maddie jokes.

"We'll just stand here and watch you sleep," Louisa says. "That won't be disturbing, will it?" She grins.

"Nothing can distract me from sleeping right now," I say, sticking my tongue out at her. "But wake me if there's any sign of trouble, okay? Or if we need to go. Or —"

"Oh my gosh, sleep already," Drew says, throwing his sweater at my head.

I grab the sweater and add it to my pillow. As I close my eyes, I can hear him chuckling, and the murmur of Maddie and Louisa chatting quietly, and Ryan snoring already. Overhead, Evelyn's and Alonso's footsteps echo as they search the upper level.

We're not safe yet, not by a long shot. But it's the safest place we've been since we escaped CMS. Even with the Alliance chasing us, I feel like we're going to make it home soon after all. I let myself relax, drifting into sleep.

And that is my biggest mistake.

Chapter 16

Something feels wrong the minute I wake up.

It's too quiet. I can still hear a couple of my friends' voices — but not enough of them.

I sit up fast, giving myself a splitting headache.

"Whoa," Louisa says. "Calm down, there's no fire." She's perched on the planter beside me, reading *Julie of the Wolves*. The light has changed — I must have slept for a few hours. The shadows of the escalators angle off in new directions, and there's an orange glow around the skylights, like the sun is close to setting.

I rub my temples and try to shake off my sleepiness. My skin is prickling. I know something's wrong.

"You look a lot friendlier when you're sleeping," Evelyn comments from the floor. She has papers spread out around her — some of them maps, others covered in scribbled notes that I don't think are hers.

"So I've been told," I say. Alonso is crouching beside Evelyn, studying one of the maps. I twist around. Ryan is still snoring on the next bench. And there's no one else in sight.

"Where's Maddie?" I demand, throwing off my sleeping bag. "And Drew?"

"They went to look for food," Louisa says. She puts down the book and frowns at the expression on my face. "What? They'll be right back."

"Don't worry; Maddie's not going to steal your boyfriend," Evelyn teases. I want to grab her papers and rip them into tiny shreds. Does she really think that's what I'm worried about?

"It's okay, Rosie," Louisa says. "I mean, we were all hungry. We're down to, like, three raisins and that jar of applesauce. And of course there's no food in here." She waggles her finger around at the empty stores. "So they're just finding us something to eat."

"They left the mall?" I cry. I grab my shoes and yank them on. "When did they leave? How long have they been gone?"

"Um." Louisa glances at the clock I stole, which is propped up on Maddie's pack beside her. "Like an hour, maybe?"

"An *hour*?" I'm already moving as I tie my hair back. "Which way did they go?"

"What's the big deal?" Louisa hops off the planter and chases after me. "They went out the door down that hall-way." She points, and I see more broken glass doors facing out onto an open-air parking lot. "Rosie, I'm sure they're being careful. They'll be back any minute."

I can't explain why it's a big deal. I can't explain why my heart is pounding or why panic is clawing around in my chest. For one thing, I don't have time. I have to find Drew and Maddie. I just know that it's not safe out there, and I wouldn't have let them go. They could have been spotted — they could have been captured — it should have been me out there, if it was anyone.

"Hey, Maddie was just trying to help," Louisa says, hurrying to keep up with me. "She said she wanted to be more brave, you know? I figure she can take care of herself."

"But she can't!" I say. "She's never been chased like this before! She doesn't know anything about escaping — how to hide, where to run when someone's after you —"

"But you do?" Louisa asks, giving me a hard look. "Why is that?" She grabs my arm and pulls me up short. "Rosie, what aren't you telling me?"

This is the closest I've come to spilling my secret, but I'm too scared for Maddie to feel any extra fear for myself. "Not now," I say, jerking my arm away. "I have to go find them."

I sprint to the door. No sign of helicopters in the pink-and-orange sunset sky. No cars out on the road that runs along the other side of the parking lot. But there's so much empty space out there. Only a few stunted trees cast lonely, thin shadows here and there across the lot. There's nowhere Drew and Maddie could have hidden if a helicopter suddenly showed up.

Louisa's footsteps crunch in the glass behind me as I step through the doorframe. I want to send her back, but I don't want to argue with her, and I know she won't go. I scan the row of buildings across the road. It's a smaller highway than the one Gladys was on. I don't know where Drew and Maddie would have expected to find food out here. They should have waited until dark, when we were all traveling together. *I* would have found them food. I would have done it safely.

"There!" Louisa says, pointing. Two figures are running along the road toward us, still several yards away. I can see Maddie's long brown hair flying out from the slower runner.

"Doesn't look like they found any food," Evelyn says from behind us, and I jump. I was too focused on the outside to hear her coming.

194

"That's fine, as long as they make it back safely," I say, biting my nails. It's a huge relief to see them, unharmed and, as far as I can tell, not being chased. But they're so exposed. I lean forward, wishing for them to run faster.

The two figures turn into the parking lot and jog in our direction. Maddie spots us in the doorway and waves with a big smile. Drew looks pretty cheerful, too. That's not going to last long once I get him inside and give him a piece of my mind. From now on, the rule is: no crazy missions without me.

I'm not just being bossy and controlling, although everyone might see it that way. I know I can handle the risks better than anyone else. What I can't handle is the idea of something happening to one of them — something like what happened to Wren — not when I could prevent it.

Louisa waves back. Suddenly her hand freezes in the air. I hear it at the same time: the roar of an engine starting up.

Maddie and Drew look back over their shoulders. We all see the headlights suddenly blaze brightly in an alley across the road. A truck shoots out from its hiding spot and barrels toward us, driving straight over the curb and the patches of unkempt grass.

This isn't the rusty old supply truck Gladys was driving. This is a sleek military machine, and the men hanging out the window are all brandishing guns.

My sneakers are pounding across the pavement before I can think. I don't know what my plan is, but I'm hoping I can distract the soldiers in the truck long enough for the others to escape.

Maybe Drew has the same thought, because he shoves Maddie toward the mall and runs at the truck, waving his arms.

Everything happens so fast.

The truck swerves around Drew. The soldiers barely even glance at him.

196

I'm too far away.

I'm running as fast as I can, but I'm too far away.

Two men leap out of the back of the truck. Black masks hide their faces. Maddie shrieks as they grab her around her waist. She kicks and fights and struggles, but they pin her arms and legs.

"Maddie!" Louisa screams, and I think I do, too.

I'm too far away!

They fling Maddie into the back of the truck and jump in after her.

I hear the door slam. I can still hear her screaming.

I'm almost there, but I'm too late. The truck's tires squeal as it U-turns, close enough to blast a wave of exhaust into my face. I see cold blue eyes over one of the masks in the front seat, looking straight at me as the truck wheels away.

But they don't stop for me. They don't stop for Louisa or Evelyn, running out of the mall behind me. They don't stop for Drew as he tries to jump in front of them again.

They swerve right around him and peel out of the parking lot, roaring off down the road.

I fall to my knees on the asphalt, pressing my hands to my face.

I've broken my promise to myself. I'm crying.

And Maddie is gone.

Chapter 17

"Rosie? Rosie, it's okay." Drew drops to his knees beside me and puts his arms around me.

"It is *not* okay!" I shove him away and he flails for balance. "This is your fault! They caught Maddie and it's all your fault!" All my fears about him come flooding back. Maybe he betrayed us after all. Maybe Maddie didn't watch him like I did, and he managed to sneak off to call the Alliance down on us. They clearly didn't want him — the truck went right around him twice.

"I know," Drew says. His voice sounds shaky and his glasses are crooked. "I tried — I'm sorry —"

"You should have tried harder!" I yell. "You should have saved her! You shouldn't have taken her out here in the first place! What were you thinking?" I shove his chest again and he falls backward, scraping his hands on the pavement.

But even as I'm blaming him, running through all my suspicions again, I realize I don't believe it's true. Not after everything we've been through. He screwed up, taking her with him, but I can't believe he meant for her to get caught. I wipe my eyes with my sleeves, trying to shove three years' worth of tears back into my face.

Louisa and Evelyn are standing above us now, looking shell-shocked. I turn away from them, rubbing my face, and see Alonso and Ryan running out of the mall toward us.

"Who took her? Were they Alliance?" Evelyn blurts. "Why didn't they take us? What's going to happen to her? Where will they —"

"Evelyn, SHUT UP!" Louisa yells. Evelyn's eyes go wide and her mouth snaps shut.

Louisa buries her face in her hands. I want to get up and hug her, but I'm too mad at them all for letting Maddie go, and I'm so furious at myself for falling asleep and not watching them, and I'm so frustrated that no matter what I do, I can't control everything and make it all work out.

It's crazy how upset I am. Three days ago, I didn't even like Maddie. I would have left her behind in the woods if I'd had a choice.

But now . . . now it feels like losing Wren all over again.

"Maybe they weren't Alliance," Ryan says. "Maybe they were on our side, and once they figure out who she is, they'll take her home."

"Not without an ID bracelet," I say. "Who'll believe her? They'll think she's — she's —"

"Like you," Drew says quietly. He pushes himself up to sit cross-legged a few feet away from me. I nod. Somehow it doesn't surprise me that he's figured it out.

"What?" Evelyn says. "What do you mean?"

I breathe in and out, shaky, ragged breaths. "There's something I haven't told you guys." I wrap my fingers around my wrist where my bracelet used to be. It's a stupid time for a confession, but it's as if the words are spilling out of me like the tears, pent up for so long that I can't stop them when they finally all burst out. "I'm here illegally. We — my family — we snuck into the US three years ago, after a tsunami wiped out our town in Mexico and my sister ran away."

"But —" Louisa looks even more shocked. "But that's a war crime!"

"I know," I say. "If anyone caught us, we could be deported — and that's the best-case scenario. The War means every illegal immigrant could be a spy for the Alliance. We're not," I say hurriedly. "But the government could treat us that way. It would be awful."

"That could happen to Maddie," Louisa whispers. "Without ID — they might just throw her in a prison camp and leave her there. We wouldn't even know how to find her."

"Why'd your parents risk it?" Drew asks me.

"We were looking for Wren," I say. "The Resistance helped us get into the country, and they said they'd try to find her." I shift my shoulders and push my hair out of my face. "We couldn't stay in Mexico, anyway. Our home was completely destroyed."

Memories wash over me: Wren's face as the ocean was suddenly sucked away, running away from the beach hand in hand, watching from the hills as the wave swamped over our home. Bodies floating out to sea. Water reaching from horizon to horizon. One of my orange sandals, carried away by the fierce grasp of the flood. The sodden mess of wood and brick that was left behind where my house used to be.

Wren was always talking about climate change and going out to save the world. That was how she met Ivan: he'd come down to Mexico with Greenpeace to help clean up our beaches after the latest oil spill. Or at least, that was what he told us. He must have told her something else — that he was with the Resistance, and together they could make a difference, if she'd run away to the States with him. And then they disappeared.

My parents' money got us into the country, with the help of the Resistance, but no matter how rich we were, it didn't help us find Wren, and it never made us feel safe.

"I've been terrified every minute for the last three years," I say. "It's kind of a relief to tell someone. I'm sorry I had to lie to you for so long."

I guess I expect them all to hate me now, so I don't know what to think when Louisa kneels and hugs me. But that's nothing compared to my surprise when Evelyn does the same.

"We don't care where you were born," Louisa says firmly. "You're our friend."

Alonso and Ryan crouch beside us. I glance up at Alonso's face, so much like the boys I grew up with. "I wondered if you were — I mean, if you might also —"

Alonso shakes his head. "Born here, although we moved around a lot. But it hasn't been easy since the War started — I get stopped and searched all the time. It's scary enough when you don't have anything to hide. . . . I can't imagine what it's been like for you."

"That's how you knew about the ID bracelets," Evelyn says, snapping her fingers.

"And that's what you meant about knowing how to escape," Louisa adds.

"We nearly got caught a couple of times while we were crossing the border," I say. I ball my hands into fists, rubbing them against my cargo pants. "I remember how scared I was. That must be how Maddie feels now. We have to *do* something!"

"I am really sorry," Drew says again. He sounds even more devastated than the rest of us. I lean forward and take one of his hands.

"We'll fix this," I say. "I know you tried to save her. I saw you trying to draw them away." He's not like Ivan. I can trust him. I squeeze his hand, hoping he can feel that.

"They really wanted Maddie," Evelyn pipes up. "Did you guys notice that? They ignored the rest of us and just went after her." She fingers her braids, frowning thought-fully. "I wonder why. There must be something special about her that we don't know."

"No way," Louisa says. "I know everything about Maddie. We've been best friends since we were five. Trust me, if there were anything about her that would interest the Alliance, I'd know."

"Yeah, they probably just grabbed her because she was the easiest to take," Ryan says.

Evelyn sets her jaw stubbornly. I know her theories are usually a little far-fetched, but part of me thinks she might be on to something, for once. It was weird how the truck went straight for Maddie. But why her? Her parents aren't rich. She doesn't even know where they are. What could the Alliance possibly want her for?

"So what do we do now?" Alonso asks.

"I guess we keep going — get back to Chicago, find our parents, and tell them what happened," Ryan says. "Right?" He sounds like he's not really thrilled about that plan.

"We can't just abandon her," Louisa says.

"I agree," I say. "I don't know about you guys, but I won't be able to handle it when they pat us on the head and make us stay inside after dark while they do nothing. I think we have to be the ones to help her. I think we're the only ones who can. We have to."

"We'll find her ourselves," Drew agrees. I get to my feet and pull him up beside me. As the others stand up and brush themselves off, I straighten his glasses and he traces his fingers across my cheek. His face doesn't look smug to me anymore. He might know all my secrets, but now I don't mind. I'm actually kind of glad.

I look up at the sky, where the orange and pink is fading into dark purple, and heavy gray clouds are starting to roll in, smothering the early stars.

Maddie is one of us. We're not going to leave her out there on her own.

Our flight toward home will have to wait.

It's time for a rescue.

207

What will happen tomorrow?
Read on for a preview of
Tomorrow Girls #3: With the Enemy.

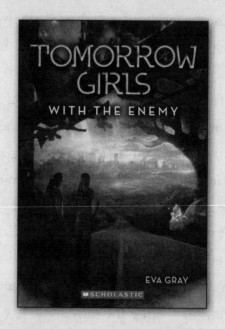

We divide up the food evenly and start eating. I put a
berry in my mouth and bite down and it explodes with
a burst of tart juice on my tongue. I eat another as I peel
off the green skin of one of the nuts and edge the tip of
my CMS–issued knife in the crack to pry it open. It takes

work but the nut inside is crunchy with a taste somewhere between an almond and a peanut.

Maybe it's because I'm starving but I think these are probably the best nuts and berries I have ever eaten in my life, possibly the best ones in the world. For five minutes the only noise in the snack bar is the sound of shells cracking open.

Until Louisa says, "I wish they'd taken me, too." She puts down her knife and pushes away the rest of her nuts. I'm sitting next to her so I can hear the trembling in her voice.

"Who?" I ask, setting down my knife and turning toward her.

"The people in the — what did Helen and Troy call it — Rover. The people who took Maddie." She looks around at all of us and there are tears in the corners of her eyes. I slide off my stool and give her a hug.

"I hate thinking of her there alone," she says into my shoulder. "Why did they only take *her*?"

My throat feels like it's closing up.

Louisa pulls away from me but keeps hold of my wrist as she repeats, "Why?"

I can't move. I can't breathe. I can't tell them.

"Maybe because she's the smallest," Ryan says after a moment.

"That would make her the easiest to control," Alonso confirms. "That makes sense."

"And to feed," Rosie points out. She brushes the shells from her hands and touches Louisa lightly on the arm.

"Seriously, what if they'd taken Ryan?" Alonso puts in then. "They'd waste all their ransom money on food."

Louisa relaxes the hold on my wrist and gives a little smile and says, "I guess."

Drew sits up straighter. "The truth is, we might not know why. But at least now we have some idea of who took her, and where. Right, Evelyn?"

I discover I've been holding my breath. "Right," I say. "We have something to go from."

Disaster is averted. Eating recommences. Boys are strange but at this moment I am really glad they're here.

We are filling Alonso and Ryan in on what Helen and Troy told us when there's a tapping on the boards over one of the windows.

Followed by a low moaning.

Instinctively, we all turn off our flashlights. What you can't see you can't shoot.

"That's just wind," Rosie says, but next to me I feel her tense. My heart starts to beat faster and my palms get clammy.

Something thuds on the roof of the building, and there's a sound like feet skittering over it.

"What's that?" I whisper to Rosie in the dark, my heart racing.

"Tree branches?" she whispers back, not sounding completely sure.

That's when a voice outside demands, "Who?"

I jump to my feet, panting. "That is not the wind, that is someone —"

"*Who who*," the voice calls again. An owl. It's an owl.

Everyone else starts to laugh but it takes some time

for the "All clear, just nature" message to get from my brain to my heart, which continues running a race in my chest. Our flashlights click back on.

Drew pulls himself to his feet. "Look, I'm feeling much better. This place is creepy and I think we should keep moving."

The speed with which everyone else leaps up and starts shoving things in their packs shows how much they agree.

We skirt the edge of the pavement toward a driveway Ryan and Alonso saw before which we're pretty sure must lead to the highway. It's long past 7:30 — which means long past curfew — but since it's night we decide to risk walking on the road, where we'll make better time. The chance of there being anyone driving on it, with the current price of gas, is remote, and even if there were someone, we'd hear their engine or see their lights long before they could see us in the dark.

Drew and Louisa lead the way, with Ryan and Alonso behind them. Rosie hangs back to walk next to me.

"Do you really think Maddie is in that place that Helen and Troy came from?" she asks.

"It sounds like she was picked up by the same people, and the tire tracks headed to Chicago," I say. The temperature has dropped and our breath is making little clouds in the air. "Why?"

"I don't know." Rosie kicks a stone from the road. "I thought Helen was mostly talking to stall until Alonso and Ryan came back with the food once you pointed out we didn't have any."

My fingers tighten around the straps of my backpack. "I shouldn't have done that. I was just worried they were going to hurt you."

Rosie pats me on the arm. "Believe me, I'm not complaining. You handled that great."

"Really?" I say. I instantly feel a thousand times better.

"Yeah." But then she purses her lips. "Although I do think it's funny that you can talk down two crazy hostage takers and save my life, but you're afraid of an owl."

"I didn't know it was an owl!" I object. "Besides, you were scared, too."

"Nuh-uh," Rosie says.

"Uh-huh," I reply.

"Do I need to separate you two?" Alonso turns around to ask. "I thought I heard my name and I wanted to let you know it's okay if you want to tell me how handsome and brave and quietly brilliant I am to my face — you don't have to do it behind my back."

"Same goes for me," Ryan says. "Although my brilliance isn't quiet."

"Duly noted," Rosie says, gesturing for them to return to their own conversation. She rolls her eyes at their backs, then says to me, "Assuming the school is real, how do we find it?"

"Even though Helen was lying, I have the sense that they told us more than they meant to." I try to think of how to explain what I mean. "When Troy talked about the Phoenix, that all seemed completely real."

"Helen said he made it all up," Rosie points out.

"Which practically guarantees that it's true," I say. I am starting to get excited. "Do you know that feeling where you're close to uncovering an answer or solving a problem but you can't quite touch it?"

Rosie nods slowly. "I do. Remember when we were in that prison camp, the one we broke into?"

I give her my most innocence-filled look. "No, I'm afraid I have totally forgotten about the time when we broke into a prison camp. What was it, two days ago?"

She makes a face at me. "I'm serious. When we were there I — I felt like I was close to finding my sister, Wren. Like maybe if I stayed I could figure out what happened to her after Ivan betrayed her, where she ended up. Is that the same?"

"No," I say. "That's much worse." And then it hits me just how bad. I turn toward her. "You gave up that chance to save the rest of us."

She shrugs, not meeting my eyes. "What choice did I have? You would never have gotten anywhere without me." Her tone is light but I can tell it hurts. "Of course, maybe you would have been better off. Maybe then Maddie would still be here."

I stop walking and pull on her pack until she stops, too, and turns to face me. "You have to cut that out," I tell her. "There was nothing you could have done to keep Maddie from being kidnapped. Whoever took her knew who she was and knew what they were doing. The only thing that could have gone differently was that you could have gotten hurt. Is that what you want?"

She stares at me wide-eyed and I realize everyone else has stopped in the middle of the road and is staring at me, too. Silence falls hard and heavy.

"She's right," Louisa says, coming to stand next to Rosie. "There was nothing you could do."

"Maddie wouldn't want you to beat yourself up," I point out.

Rosie flips her hand in the air, brushing this aside. "People always say that."

That makes me angry — I am not *people* — and

maybe that's why I say, "In this case it happens to be true. Maddie wouldn't want you to be throwing a pity party for yourself because you lost her the same way you lost Wren." I hear Rosie's sharp intake of breath but I don't stop. "She would want you to focus on what needs to happen next, not what happened before. She'd want you, the strongest leader in our group, to help find her. And if we can find Maddie, we can find your sister."

Rosie's jaw is tight and she takes three breaths before she says, "Do you really think so? Do you really think that's true?"

"I do," I say. If I'm not going to mention that I think Maddie might be (as good as) dead, there's no reason to mention I have no idea how to find Wren.

POISON APPLE BOOKS

The Dead End

This Totally Bites!

Miss Fortune

Now You See Me...

Midnight Howl

Her Evil Twin

THRILLING. BONE-CHILLING.
THESE BOOKS HAVE BITE!